The Wild Animal Kids Club – Book 1

I...am...Cheetah!

~*The Gift*~

Stephanie J. Teer

An *imprint* of Graphic Brains Press

Copyright © 2014 Stephanie J. Teer

Ordering Information: Quantity sales. Special discounts are available on quantity purchases by corporations, associations, and others.

For details, contact the publisher at

info@graphicbrains.com

or

Graphic Brains Press
P.O . Box 17492
Reno, NV 89521

ISBN-10: 0692269592
ISBN-13: 978-0692269596

First Edition

Art and Photo Credits

Art Design by Nicole Medrano
5-Safari Park Sign;9-Sandbox;12-Gabby holding zebra;16-Muddy zebra; 84-cheetahs running with soccer balls;87-cheetah stalking balls; 92-cheetah in soccer net;105-cheetah chewing on shoe; 116-playground;129-Safari Park Sign;8,32,50,58,90,104,112,blank page after 140-Paw Prints

Bigstock.com Photo & Art Credits
Title Page- Perysty;4-Gary Tognoni;19-Gail Johnson;20-SURZ; 26-lamnee;27-Monkeybusinessimages, zurijeta, alenkasm; 28-Bruce Jones; 39-kentoh;67-matejh, Jo McCarthy, Wilma; 119-kentoh;126-127-Perysty; 133-jannoon028,Alexey Pushkin, Benchart, elein, insima, bestdesign36;

Photo & Art Design Credits: 132-David's Door
Door Illustration-Nicole Medrano; Keep Out Sign-David Teer; Cheetah Open Mouth-Tim Torell; Enter at risk sign-PIXXart/Bigstock.com; cheetah speed limit sign-Pixabay

Real Cheetahs! Real Facts! Photo Credits
142-Tim Torell;143-Wilma/Bigstock.com;144-Adrio/Bigstock.com; 145-Traverlspic/Bigstock.com

Character photos converted to cartoons by Fiverr Artist: Margana
Pages 27, 127 &148

Cover
Design by Fiverr Artist -mrdani4u
Golden Portal- kentoh/Bigstock.com;Cheetah-16987604/iStock.com

Wildlife Hero Spotlight and Book: *"A Future for Cheetahs"*
Images: Courtesy of The Cheetah Conservation Fund (CCF)

Facebook Page Photo Credits
Cheetah-Tim Torell; Lion, Panda, Tiger- egal/bigstock.com; Zebra-David Teer; Elephants & Meerkat-EcoShot/Bigstock.com; West African Crowned Crane-David Teer; Wolf-hkuchera/Bigstock.com; European Bee Eater- mirceab/Bigstock.com;

Animal Illustration Design Credits

Bigstock.com
40-Julian W;41-Four Oaks;47-Four Oaks;57-Four Oaks; 61-Jessamyn Smallenburg;65-outdoorsman;70-Four Oaks; 87-Travelerpics; 140-Lynn_B

iStock.com
42-12560400;77-24824813;80-12431188;92-4945542; 97-3312986;101-17953125;105-12234693

123RF.com
43-Jason Prince/7974376;54-Duncan Noakes/5760005;84-dndavis/672051;109-Jason Prince/7974345; 110-Francois Gagnon/15552796

Table of Contents

This book is dedicated to

Nathan and David
~My two most precious gifts in life~

And...

to the wildlife warriors
who dedicate their lives to saving
the most elegant and fastest land animal
on the earth—the cheetah.

Thank you to my family and friends for their constant support. I couldn't have done it without you.

Georgie, your love and absolute faith in me always keeps me going.

Mom, thanks for always believing in me.

Also, a big thank you goes out to my kid beta readers for sharing their thoughts about the Wild Animal Kids Club series.
You're all awesome!

Nathan Teer
David Teer
Hunter Aycock
Blake Aycock
Khloe Patrick
Alyssa Schricker
Ali Barrios

Park Day

Fridays were magical for nine-year-old Gabby Rose Cedillo. Why? Because it was park day, of course. Actually, it was a 'Long Beach Kids' park day. And as far as she was concerned, it was the best day of the week.

Every Friday, kids could hang out with friends, play sports, and even sign up for some fun park classes. There was 'Art in the Park' with Ms. Tammy, 'Kids Knit' with Ms. Billie, 'Science Maniacs' with Mr. Jasper, and a bunch more.

Gabby wiggled around in her seat as her mom drove past the ocean on Pacific Coast Highway. She turned to talk to her eleven-year-old brother, Nathan, but he was plugged in listening to music on his cell phone. Nathan only came to the park to practice basketball with his surfing buddies.

"Whatcha listening to?" Gabby asked.

No answer. Nathan just hummed softly and kept tapping the basketball.

Gabby frowned. *Those are some pretty good earphones*, she thought. She gently poked him.

Nothing. Then Gabby got a better idea. She reached up and yanked on a few strands of his dark brown hair.

"Ow!"

Yep, that got his attention.

"Gabbs, what was that for?" Nathan pulled out his earphones.

"It was the only way to get your attention," Gabby said, grinning. "I think you were daydreaming that you were a rock and roll star again."

"What? I...I don't do that," Nathan stammered.

"Ya-huh," Gabby nodded. "I've seen you in your room listening to music and playing your guitar with your eyes closed."

Nathan sighed. "You're supposed to knock before you come in, you know."

Gabby smiled sweetly. "I did knock, but *somebody* was too busy rocking out." Gabby closed her eyes and pretended to sing into an invisible microphone.

"Ha...ha. You think you're so cute," Nathan said. "I think *somebody* is about to get tickled."

Nathan dropped his basketball and attacked his sister with tickles.

Gabby shrieked and screamed with laughter.

"Excuse Me!" A voice from the backseat shouted.

Nathan stopped tickling his little sister and looked back at his ten-year-old brother, David. David ran his hand through his wavy, light brown hair like he always did when he was annoyed.

"Oh, you were so quiet. I almost forgot you existed." Nathan grinned.

"Very funny." David wasn't amused. He held up his mom's tablet. "I'm trying to watch my favorite show, if you two don't mind."

Gabby twisted around in her seat. "What are you watching?"

"*Predators on the Hunt*," David replied.

"Which predator is on the hunt this week?" asked Nathan. "My favorite is the gray wolf."

"Mine's the Sumatran tiger," Gabby added.

All three kids were crazy excited about wild animals. From tiny insects to humongous elephants, they loved them all. The Cedillo family came from a long line of wildlife veterinarians. Respect for every living creature was simply a way of life for Gabby and her brothers.

"This week it's the cheetah," David said.

Gabby's eye's lit up. "I really like the cheetahs!"

David grinned. Gabby might like them, but no one loved cheetahs as much as he did. "I was just getting to the part where the vultures swoop in to steal the gazelle from the cheetah," he said.

David turned the tablet toward them.

Nathan frowned. "Why doesn't the cheetah just attack the vultures? They're just birds."

David rolled his eyes. "How can you be a Cedillo and *not* know this stuff? Cheetahs are passive animals. The only reason they attack prey is for food. They don't fight other animals."

"Yep. He's right," Gabby agreed. "And vultures are huge. When they steal food, they do it in a big pack."

David shook his head. "No! A group of vultures eating is called a *wake*. Trust me. They are definitely not called a pack."

"Well…that's a dumb name. Of course they're awake," Gabby said. "How could they eat if they were asleep? Duh!"

David just rolled his eyes. He gave up.

4

"Kids, we're here," their mom called back. She parked in front of the tall wooden sign at Safari Park.

At twenty feet high, the grand entrance looked like it belonged in a zoo, not just a local park. An artist who had traveled all over Africa had carefully carved the wild animals into the enormous sign.

As soon as the van stopped, Nathan jumped out. "Mom, I'll be at the basketball courts. Later, gators!"

Gabby giggled. "After while, crocodile!"

"Ya know, that sounds really dumb," David said.

"Na-uh."

David nodded. "Uh, yeah it does. Trust me, no one says that anymore. It's like…ancient."

Gabby frowned. "Dad still says it and he's not…*ancient.*"

"Are you sure about that?"

"David, sweetheart," his mom called out as she closed her door. "Did you just call your dad old?"

David pointed to himself. "Who me? No way!" Technically he'd said ancient…not old.

Gabby unzipped her backpack and took out a plush zebra that her nana had just sent from Kenya, Africa. Her grandparents traveled all over the world rescuing endangered animals. They had just left Kenya and were on their way to a country called Namibia.

Gabby had brought the new zebra to show to her five-year-old reading buddy, Lucy. She was a cute kid and loved zebras as much as Gabby did.

David grabbed his backpack and headed toward the park. "Mom, I'm gonna go find Dorian."

"Remember," his mom said, "no scaring the girls with any bugs or frogs today."

David chuckled as he walked off. "C'mon, Mom. Do I look like the sort of kid that would freak out the girls in the *dorky* knitting club?"

"I mean it, David!"

But David didn't hear her. He'd sprinted off to find his best friend, Dorian.

Gabby slipped her backpack on and pulled her light brown curls free from the straps. She looked around for her best friend, Cassidy. "Mom, do you see Cass?"

"Oh, I just remembered," her mom said. "Cassidy got the stomach flu. Her mom texted me this morning."

Gabby's shoulders drooped. No Cassidy?

"I'll be by the hippo tables if you need me," her mom said. "And watch out for puddles, sweetie. It rained quite a bit yesterday."

"Okay, Mom." Gabby sighed and walked off. Park days just weren't the same without her best friend. Cassidy just always had a way of making park days a bit more...magical.

But today, things would definitely not be the same.

Today would not be so *magical*.

Today, a bully would change Gabby's life forever.

I…am…Cheetah!

The Bully

Gabby walked into Safari Park and searched for Lucy. Some of the kids sat on the giraffe swings, while others climbed the rhino rocks. Ms. Tammy walked around her art table, setting out paint brushes and glitter for her class. But there was no sign of Lucy.

Gabby headed toward the safari sandbox. Sometimes Lucy went there with her two-year-old brother, Tommy. She spotted Tommy's dump truck at the edge of the sandbox, so they had to be close by.

As she scanned the park, Gabby noticed the Strikers soccer team. The girls were practicing on the big field next to crocodile pond. The Strikers were some of the most serious soccer players Gabby had ever seen.

Madison McKinley, their team captain, was always barking orders to run faster and kick the ball farther. Cassidy had said that the Strikers had never lost a game since Madison had become team captain.

Wow, those girls are so lucky, Gabby thought.

Gabby wanted to be in a club or on a team more than anything. She'd tried to join Ms. Billie's knitting club. But Gabby's version of a knitted sock wouldn't fit any human foot on this planet.

Maybe I could be a Striker, she thought. But she wasn't very athletic and didn't know how to play soccer. That could be a *slight* problem.

Then Gabby remembered when her dad had coached Nathan's soccer team. During the games, her dad had let Gabby chase the balls that went outside the field. He'd said that she was the fastest ball girl in the league. Okay, maybe she'd been the *only* ball girl in the league, but she was definitely fast.

That's it! Gabby thought. *I could be a ball girl.*

Gabby got so excited that she forgot all about finding Lucy. She even forgot about the zebra she was holding. She sprinted toward crocodile pond as fast as she could. She couldn't wait to surprise the Strikers with her new idea.

When Gabby reached the girls, Madison was just about to kick a soccer ball into the right corner of the net.

Gabby ran up and yelled, "Hi, guys!"

Madison missed and glared at Gabby as she whipped her long blonde hair behind her. "You made me miss, Shrimp!"

"Um...sorry about that," Gabby said meekly.

All the girls stopped kicking their balls and began walking toward Gabby, with Madison in the lead.

"Listen, Shrimp, you interrupted our practice," Madison said. "You know my park rule. When we're practicing, little kids are not allowed back here."

"I didn't mean to interrupt your practice, but I had a really great idea and I just had to tell you."

Madison folded her arms. "What is it?"

Gabby took a big, deep breath before she spoke. "I figured out how I could be a Striker, too!"

"How? You don't even know how to play soccer." Madison scowled. "Besides, this club is for eleven-year-olds *only*. Not dumb little nine-year-olds."

"I know," Gabby said, "but I'm a really superfast runner. So, maybe I could chase the balls when you practice. I could be your...ball girl!"

Silence.

Some of the Strikers looked away, not wanting to face Gabby. Gabby thought the girls actually looked like they felt sorry for her.

Madison finally spoke. "You can't just chase balls to be a Striker, Dork-ess! You have to be able to *play* soccer. Don't you know anything?"

Gabby was silent. Maybe it wasn't such a great idea after all.

Madison saw the toy zebra that Gabby was holding and got a nasty idea. "So, you wanna be a ball girl…do you?"

Gabby didn't say or do anything. Now she wasn't sure what she wanted.

Madison walked up and snatched the zebra out of Gabby's hand. "Aww...look how cute, ladies. The animal geek still likes to play with her little stuffed animals."

A few of the girls laughed and smirked.

Gabby could feel her cheeks getting red. She wanted to tell them that she was sharing her zebra with her reading buddy, just to be nice. She wanted to tell them...*so what* if she liked animals. But she didn't say a single word.

Madison tossed the zebra up in the air and caught it. "So, Shrimp, if you wanna be the ball girl, then you have to be able to catch. Why don't we practice with this little guy?"

Now Gabby was getting scared and a little mad. "Um...that's okay. Can I please just have my zebra back?"

"Nope. You wanted to be a Striker, so now you get to try out." Madison held the zebra up above her head. "I'll throw your baby toy, and if you can catch him, then maybe you can be on the team."

"That's okay. Please just give it back and I'll go." Gabby had changed her mind. She didn't want to be part of this team at all. Not now...not ever!

One of the girls who actually felt sorry for Gabby spoke up. "C'mon, Maddy, just give it back to her."

"*NO!* She broke the rules. Now she has to pay." Madison glared at Gabby. "Get ready to run, Shrimp."

Gabby didn't move.

Madison pulled the zebra's legs apart. "Unless you want this guy back in pieces, I suggest you...RUN NOW!"

Nathan was practicing his layup shots when he heard Madison yell. He peered out through the tall wire fence and spotted his little sister.

"What the...?" he whispered to himself. Why was Madison holding Gabby's zebra? And why was Gabby running? Then he saw what was about to happen.

Oh no...! No, no, no.

"Coach, I'll be right back!" Nathan exploded out of the basketball courts.

As he raced toward Gabby, he saw the zebra go flying way above her head. The brand new plush zebra landed in a dirty, muddy puddle.

Nathan...was too late.

Muddy Stripes

Gabby stood next to the muddy zebra in shock. She looked up and saw Madison laughing. One girl even gave Madison a high-five, but most of the others shook their heads sadly and ran back to their soccer balls.

"Gabbs! Are you okay?" Nathan gasped as he ran up to her.

"I...I didn't know what to do," Gabby whispered.

"I'm gonna go talk to those dumb girls," he said. He started to leave, but Gabby grabbed his arm.

"Please don't," she pleaded. "Please, Nathan. Don't say anything to them. Okay?"

"No, Gabbs. It's not right. Kids are not allowed to bully. It's our number one rule for Long Beach Kids."

"But I don't want anyone to know what happened," she said softly. "The other kids...they might laugh."

Nathan crouched down next to his little sister. Her light brown curls blew in the wind, covering part of her face as she kept her eyes on the grass.

Nathan knew that Gabby wasn't only upset. She was also embarrassed by what had just happened.

Nathan sighed. "Okay, I won't tell." He reached over and picked up the brand new zebra from the large puddle. It didn't look so new now.

The sad looking zebra was completely drenched. Thin soggy blades of grass and large clumps of mud covered his entire body.

"We can rinse your zebra off at the fountain if you want," Nathan said.

Gabby shook her head. "That's okay. I can do it." She took her zebra and glanced back. Madison was watching her.

Nathan gently turned his sister toward him. "Don't look at her, Gabbs. Just ignore her. She is *so* not worth it. Got me?"

Gabby nodded and whispered, "Thanks for not telling. You're the best."

Nathan pulled his little sister into a huge bear hug. He didn't care who was watching. "You're the best too," he whispered back. "Don't ever forget it."

Gabby tried to fight back tears. But the tears won and a few slid down both her cheeks. She swatted them away as fast as she could. Gabby was so mad and so embarrassed at the same time. She didn't know which was worse.

Nathan felt awful. "Sis, what can I do?" He squeezed her hand. "Anything! Just tell me."

Gabby squeezed his hand back and gave her big brother a small smile. Normally, Nathan just had a way of making everything all right. But not today. Today *no one* could make her feel better. "It's okay. I gotta go. See ya."

"See ya," Nathan replied sadly.

He watched Gabby as she quickly rinsed the mud and grass off her zebra. Then he saw his sister walk over and say something to their mom. Their mom got up and took Gabby to the minivan.

Nathan clenched his fists together. He was so mad! How could Madison be so mean to someone so kind? Gabby was nice to everyone, especially to the little kids in the park. She was always so patient with them, and they adored her for it.

He didn't understand it. He'd known Madison for a long time and she'd always been pretty nice. But ever since Madison had become the team captain of the Strikers, she'd started bullying the younger kids in the park.

Nathan was still angry when he saw his little brother running toward him.

"Nathan, Nathan! What happened to Gabbs?" David asked. "She's sitting in the van and she looks like she's been crying. She won't tell Mom anything. And what happened to her zebra? It looks like someone dragged it through the mud."

"Promise not to tell?"

"For Gabby…big time. I promise," David said.

Nathan told him everything.

David turned and scowled at the Strikers practicing on the field. "Dumb, toad-faced girls." David glared at Madison. "Nathan, I've got a plan."

"What do you mean, a plan?"

"Dorian and I found a baby garden snake by the rhino rocks. He's holding it for me. Let's sneak up and put it in Madison's duffle bag."

"I thought Mom told you to stop scaring all the girls." Nathan shook his head. "Nah, we have to do something different for Gabbs."

David frowned, a bit disappointed that he wouldn't be able to carry out his *'snake in the bag'* plan.

"Besides," Nathan said, "that won't make Gabby feel any better."

"It'll sure make *me* feel a whole lot better," David said.

Nathan looked down and noticed David holding his mom's tablet. "What are you doing with that?"

"I wanted to show Dorian the pictures that Grandpa emailed yesterday." David handed the tablet to his brother. "He found two male cheetahs when he went to Namibia. When male cheetahs form a group, it's called a coalition."

Nathan grinned. His brother knew everything there was to know about cheetahs. He swiped to the next photo.

"That's my favorite," David said. "Grandpa said that it looked like the cheetahs were playing leapfrog."

Nathan smiled as he looked at the three cheetah cubs playing together. *Three cheetah cubs*, he thought. Then Nathan remembered something. Something...magical!

"That's it!" Nathan cried.

"What's it?" David asked.

"The answer," Nathan replied firmly.

"What was the question?" David was completely confused.

"Why didn't I think of that before?" Nathan was getting excited.

David was getting annoyed. "Hellooooo...Earth to Nathan! What are you even talking about?"

Nathan's eyes lit up. "Davy, let's start a club. A secret club for animal lovers."

"That sounds pretty cool. But why does it have to be a secret?"

"Because I need to share a magical secret," Nathan replied. "And I can't do that without a secret club. Get it?"

"Um...not really," David said, still confused. Magic? What was his brother thinking? Nobody believed in magic.

"Davy, make sure you tell Dorian and Cassidy about what we're doing. They should be part of the club, don't you think?"

David nodded. "Yeah. If it's gonna be a secret club, the only person I trust is Dorian. I know Gabby feels the same way about Cassidy."

Nathan looked up and still didn't see his little sister back in the park. "Why don't you go tell Mom we're ready to go. I bet Gabbs just wants to go home."

"Okay." David dashed off.

Nathan would never forget the day he came to rescue his little sister and had been too late. But on that awful day, Nathan made a decision.

He decided that it was time to give his brother and sister a gift. A gift that would change their lives forever.

Nathan looked around and smiled.

An animal club was perfect for sharing the biggest secret ever to come to Safari Park.

Safari Park would never be the same!

Wild Animal Kids Club
(One Week Later)

Gabby and David walked into Safari Park and searched for Cassidy and Dorian. David spotted his best friend near the hippos tables where all the parents usually sat. David waved just as Dorian looked up.

Dorian ran over and greeted his friends. "Hey, guys." Dorian had short black curly hair, dark skin, and light brown eyes that sparkled with curiosity.

"Hey, Big D. What were you doing?" David asked.

Dorian was the same age as David and just a bit shorter, but everyone still called him Big D. It was a nickname, David always said, for his *humongous* brain. For a ten-year-old, Dorian was the smartest kid David had ever met.

"I was helping my mom unload the car," Dorian replied. "Where's Nathan?"

"He's already at the lion's den," David told him. "That's where we're gonna meet."

"Really? Why there?" Dorian asked.

But before David could answer, Cassidy ran up. "Hey, dudes and dudette!" Her dark green eyes lit up with laughter as she hugged her best friend.

Cassidy and Gabby had been best friends ever since they had met at Safari Park four years ago. Even though the girls were both nine, they were as different as night and day.

Gabby was girly, a bit shy, and never wanted to hurt anyone's feelings. Cassidy was all tomboy, fearless, and always said exactly what was on her mind—nice or not!

"Hey, Freckles." David grinned.

"And proud of it." Cassidy grinned right back as she playfully punched David in the arm.

"Ow!" David cried, rubbing his arm.

Cassidy rolled her eyes. "Oh please. I barely touched you, tough guy."

"Cass," Gabby said, "Nathan wants to meet in the lion's den so he can share his secret."

Cassidy pushed her long red hair away from her face. "You mean the magical secret?"

Gabby nodded. "Uh-huh."

"That's so cool," Cassidy said. "I just love magical stuff. I can't wait!"

"Oh, brother," David whispered to Dorian.

Dorian didn't say anything, but he completely agreed. He and David were science geeks and proud of it. *Magic? I don't think so*, Dorian thought. It just didn't exist as far as he was concerned.

David saw his brother standing at the entrance of the lion's den. Nathan waved and then quickly slipped inside.

Together, the four kids headed to the largest playhouse in the park.

The giant metal lion sat quietly on its two front paws. A cool ocean breeze blew through its hollow eyes and ears. The lion's back, which was covered with large open slits, allowed sunlight to sneak into the wide open space inside.

As the kids stepped through the large door under the lion's mouth, they noticed small patches of grass scattered across the dirt floor. Huge streaks of sunlight peered into the empty chamber.

"Hey, guys!" Nathan said. "Let's sit down and get started. Gabbs, did you come up with a name for the club?"

Gabby nodded. "Yeah, I did." She reached into her backpack and took out a small notecard and a map of Africa. "But first I want to read a letter from my nana. It's where I got the idea for the name." Gabby began reading.

My dearest Nathan, David, and Gabriella,

Grandpa and I have just left Namibia. We visited the Cheetah Conservation Fund Center and met Dr. Laurie Marker. She is an amazing woman.

Her love for cheetahs reminds me of how much you all love wild animals.

On our way to Botswana. Will write again, soon.

Kisses and hugs to my sweet Wild Animal Kids.

Love,
Nana and Grandpa

Gabby put the note card back into her backpack and handed the map to David.

"I think we should be called *The Wild Animal Kids*," she said. "I even made a sign with all our pictures.

"And," David began, "Gabby and I decided that our club should learn about endangered animals."

"Cool," Dorian said. "I love learning about endangered animals."

"Big D, you love learning about anything." David grinned.

Dorian grinned too. He knew that was true.

David placed the map on the ground so all the kids could see it. He'd circled the country of Namibia. "Here's where my grandparents went."

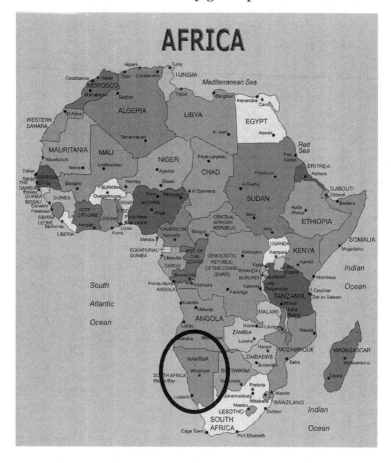

Cassidy frowned. "How do you pronounce that again?"

David spoke slowly. "nuh-MIH-bee-uh...just like it's spelled...Namibia."

"I've read that Namibia is the cheetah capital of the world," Dorian said. "There's more cheetahs there than anywhere else."

Gabby smiled. "That's because of all the work that Dr. Laurie Marker and her helpers are doing. That's what my grandpa told me."

David reached into his backpack and took out a brown leather journal and a small sketchpad. He and his sister had decided to keep notes and sketch drawings of the animals the club learned about.

"Anyway," David said, "the first animal we're gonna learn about is my favorite—the cheetah. They're the coolest animals on the planet, you know." David turned his attention to Nathan. "Okay, big brother, spill it! What's the secret?"

Nathan peered out into the park. He saw kids swinging on the giraffe swings and climbing across the monkey bars. But no one seemed interested in the lion's den today.

"I'll share the secret," Nathan said, "but this secret starts with a story."

David put his hands up. "Are you kidding me? A story? You never said anything about a story. Do you really have a secret?"

"Just be patient," Nathan said. "Story first, magical secret next. I promise."

"Sure, sure, whatever. We'll see," David said. "You know I don't believe in magic, right?"

"Trust me," Nathan said. "After today, you'll all believe in magic."

The kids settled down and sat quietly, ready for Nathan to share his story and reveal the magical secret.

Nathan took a deep breath and began his tale. "A long time ago a young man traveled all around the world to help save endangered animals," he said. "When he went to Africa, the young man loved it so much that he decided to live there. He even became a Wildlife Warrior."

"What's a Wildlife Warrior?" Dorian asked.

"Wildlife Warriors defend and protect endangered animals," Nathan explained. "It's sad, but some people-like poachers, still want to hurt and steal endangered animals."

"This guy sounds pretty brave," David said. "Poachers can be dangerous."

Nathan nodded and continued. "Then one day, the young man decided it was time to come back to the United States."

"How come?" Gabby asked.

"Well," Nathan said, "while he was there, he met a beautiful young woman traveling through Africa. She also loved wild animals and wanted to help protect them."

"Wow," Gabby said. "She loved animals, too?"

"Yep," Nathan said. "The young man fell in love with her. When she went home, he knew he had to follow. He loved Africa, but he loved *her* even more."

"Figures," David said, shaking his head. "Leave it to a girl to ruin everything."

Gabby sighed. "I think that's so romantic."

David rolled his eyes. "Of course you do."

Nathan continued. "But before the young man left Africa, he went to say goodbye to one of the tribal chiefs. The African chief held a huge celebration for the young man and gave him a very special gift."

"What was the gift?" Cassidy asked.

"A wooden box filled with beads," Nathan said.

"Beads," David said, frowning. "Why would a guy want beads?"

"You probably didn't know this, but beads are very important to people in Africa," Nathan replied.

"Really?" Cassidy asked.

Dorian answered. "Oh yeah, Nathan is right. In some African countries, beads are traded for food and livestock. In other countries, beads can show how rich a person is."

Nathan nodded. "You're right, Big D, but this African chief gave the young man a magical box filled with magical warrior beads. Beads that could change your lives...forever!"

A Magical Secret

"Nuh-uh," David said. "Now you're just messing with us?

Nathan shook his head. "No, it's true! Magical beads are given to all Wildlife Warriors. Becoming a Wildlife Warrior is a huge honor."

David frowned. "That's not what I was talking about. What do you mean...beads that can change our lives? How can a dumb bead create magic?"

Nathan sighed. "Gah! You ask a lot of questions. Are you going to let me finish the story or not?"

David crossed his arms and just rolled his eyes.

The kids sat silently waiting for Nathan to continue. The boys looked bored, still not believing in any type of magic. The girls, on the other hand, had a dreamy look in their eyes and couldn't wait to hear more.

Nathan continued. "Like I said, becoming a Wildlife Warrior is a huge honor."

"Why?" Cassidy asked.

"Because," Nathan replied, "the beads are filled with the warrior's love of all wild creatures and the courage to rescue endangered animals."

"Is that really true?" Gabby asked.

Nathan nodded. "Oh yeah. Warrior beads are given to Wildlife Warriors all over the world. The magic of the beads has to stay within their families."

"Wow," Cassidy said. "That's such a cool story."

Nathan continued. "So the young man came home and married the beautiful young woman. He gave the magical box of beads to her as a wedding present." Nathan reached into his duffle bag and pulled out a small wooden box.

An elephant made out of white crystal sat on top. Nathan lifted the lid and revealed ten glass beads. The tube-shaped beads were painted in different colors. Each one had its own special design.

Cassidy gasped. "Oh my gosh! Are those the beads?"

"Yep," Nathan said proudly.

Dorian was confused. "Why do *you* have the beads?"

Nathan smiled. This was the best part of the story. "Because...the young man who traveled around the world was our dad!"

"No way!" David cried.

Gabby gasped. "I knew Mom and Dad met in Africa, but I never knew about the beads. And now they belong to you?"

"Actually, they belong to all of us," Nathan said.

"Okay," David said, "since the story is about Mom and Dad, maybe it's not so boring. But it's still just a story. I don't think you can call that a magical secret."

Nathan grinned. "I never said that was the secret. I *said* the secret starts with a story."

David frowned. He was still confused.

"Let me show you." Nathan handed the wooden box to Gabby. "Gabbs, pick a bead."

Gabby looked in and stared at all the magical beads. How could she choose just one? They were all so beautiful.

"Don't worry, Sis," Nathan said softly. "Just pick the one that *feels* right for you."

Gabby reached in and selected a bright yellow bead with a starburst design. She took the bead and quickly showed it to Cassidy.

Nathan took the box from Gabby and gave it to David. "Go ahead, little brother. Pick one."

David spotted an amber bead with two gold and black paw prints in the middle. "I like this one the best."

Nathan felt around for the perfect bead and pulled out a light brown bead painted with dark green, wavy lines.

"Now," Nathan said, "since the club is going to learn about cheetahs today, close your eyes and imagine a real live cheetah cub."

Gabby quickly shut her eyes tight and imagined a small cheetah cub playing with flowers and butterflies.

David raised a single eyebrow. "You've got to be kidding me. You want me to pretend?"

Nathan tilted his head toward Gabby, whose eyes were still shut tight. "C'mon. Do it for Gabbs," he whispered.

David closed his eyes and imagined a cub running through the grasslands of Africa. His imaginary cub was learning how to hunt with the mother cheetah.

Nathan imagined a cheetah lying on a large rock or maybe a large termite mound in Africa. His cub was enjoying the warm African sunshine.

David opened his eyes and looked over at his best friend. Dorian frowned and quietly mouthed, *"What is going on?"*

David just shrugged. He didn't know what Nathan was up to either.

Nathan opened his eyes. "Okay," Nathan said. "Now, do what I do and repeat after me."

Nathan held the bead in both hands. "We choose to share this gift with our friends, Cassidy and Dorian."

David and Gabby held their beads with both hands and repeated Nathan's words. "We choose to share this gift with our friends, Cassidy and Dorian."

Nathan blew into his bead. "I imagine…."

David and Gabby blew into their beads. "I imagine…"

Nathan blew again. "I believe…"

David and Gabby blew again. "I believe…"

And then Nathan blew for the last time. "I…am…cheetah!"

David and Gabby blew for the last time. "I…am…cheetah!"

"Now put the beads on the ground," Nathan said.

The kids gently placed the beads on a small patch of grass. As soon as the beads touched the ground, something magical happened.

The beads started shaking back and forth, trembling on the grass.

Suddenly, sparks of bright light shot out from the three beads sitting on the ground. The lights danced and swirled in the air, moving all around the big chamber of the lion's den.

David and Dorian looked at each other with their mouths slightly open. Maybe magic did exist!

The rays of light started spinning, creating a large golden circle. Creating...a magical portal!

A thick beam of light burst out from the golden doorway and sucked the three beads right back in. A gush of wind blew through the giant lion as the swirling lights began to spin faster and faster. The kids gazed into the magical portal, wondering what would happen next.

Within seconds, a tiny paw appeared. And it was coming *through* the portal. Step-by-step the animal slowly walked out until its entire body stood in front of them.

The kids gasped in shock and awe as they stared at the magical creature. Staring back at them was a pair of beautiful, light amber eyes. The kids were gazing into the eyes of a real, living and breathing, furry cheetah cub.

The cub shook its head and stared at all the children. Hanging around the cheetah's neck was a brown leather cord with the same bead Gabby had picked from the wooden box. The starburst design glowed just slightly.

Before the kids could utter a single word, another cheetah cub jumped out and appeared before them. The cheetah studied the children and then calmly sat down in front of them.

This cheetah wore the bead that Nathan had selected. The bead's wavy green lines shimmered, glowing brightly under the cheetah's chin.

Finally, the last cheetah appeared. This cheetah jumped out ready to pounce on its next prey! But as soon as the cub saw the kids, it relaxed.

David noticed the bead hanging around the cheetah's neck. It was the same bead he'd chosen, but now the paw prints were glowing.

David looked straight at his brother with the biggest grin on the planet. "Now *that's* a secret!"

The Gift

As soon as the golden portal disappeared, the cubs' beads stopped glowing. Then all Nathan heard were gasps and giggles as the cheetah cubs began sniffing and climbing all over the kids.

The smallest cheetah slowly walked up to Gabby and stared directly at her.

The cub, still a bit scared, seemed unsure of what to do. And then the cub heard Gabby's sweet voice.

"Come here, little cheetah," Gabby called. "I'll protect you."

The frightened cub ran straight into her arms for safety.

The cub wearing David's amber bead didn't appear to be scared at all. His cheetah dashed toward him and jumped up.

"Whoa, whoa!" David cried as he put his hands up. "No prey here, little buddy." David gently grabbed his cheetah around the stomach and stroked the soft fur on his head. The small cub purred loudly.

David looked over at Nathan. "How is this even possible?" he asked. "I mean…how did the beads do this?"

Nathan shrugged. "I don't know how it all works. Mom and Dad just said the beads create a magical doorway for the animals to come in."

Nathan turned to Gabby. "So what do you think, Sis?"

Gabby felt the soft pads of her cheetah's little paws. They were covered with wispy strands of gold and black fur. "I think…I think this is the best gift I've ever got in my whole entire life!"

Nathan's cheetah walked around and sat next to Cassidy. The curious cub lifted its paw and began playing with Cassidy's long, red silky hair.

Cassidy giggled. She thought the cheetah was the cutest little cub she'd ever seen.

Dorian shook his head. This had to be a dream. He closed his eyes and then opened them. Nope. Magical furry cheetahs still there. Impossible!

"Big D, what's wrong?" David asked.

Dorian stared at the cheetah cubs and took a deep breath. "Davy, this just can't be possible. This can't be real. Right?"

"Why are you asking me?" David pointed to Nathan. "It's his secret."

Dorian looked directly at Nathan. "And where did that golden portal come from anyway? Nathan, I need answers. This can't be real."

"Sorry, Dorian," Nathan said. "All I know is what my mom and dad told me."

"What did they tell you?" Cassidy asked as she stroked the cheetah sitting next to her.

Nathan thought for a second. "They said the real magic comes from a child's imagination. There's nothing stronger than that."

Dorian shook his head. There had to be another explanation.

Nathan paused and thought again. "My mom said that the magic also comes from our heart, like our love for wild animals. But most important, it comes from believing that *anything* is possible."

Feeling very satisfied with his answer, Nathan smiled at Dorian. "Does that help?"

"Absolutely…*not*." Dorian groaned and fell back.

David's cub immediately pounced on Dorian's stomach. The cheetah licked Dorian's nose and cheeks with his rough grainy tongue.

"Ew!" Dorian quickly covered his face with his arms.

David laughed. "Things feeling pretty real now, Big D?"

Gabby's cub was curled up on her lap and purring loudly. Her front paws were nestled in Gabby hands. The small cub felt safe and protected.

"Gabbs, that little guy really likes you," Cassidy said.

Gabby picked up her cheetah and looked under her tummy. "You mean this little *girl*."

Soon all the cubs were getting picked up and turned over.

David reached over and lifted the cub off Dorian's stomach. "Mine's a boy," David said.

"And this little cheetah is a boy, too," Cassidy said. "David, how old do you think the cubs are?"

David glanced around and studied the cheetahs. "They're pretty small. And they still have a bunch of hair sticking up on their neck and back. I bet they're about three to four months old."

"You guys might want to name them while they're here," Nathan suggested.

"I already did," Gabby said. "My cub's name is *Sunshine*, because that's what I imagined. A cub playing with butterflies and flowers in the sunshine."

David remembered what he'd imagined. "My cheetah was running, probably chasing his prey. I'm calling mine, *Chase*."

Cassidy looked at Nathan's cub and touched the bead. "Nathan, what should we call your cheetah?"

Nathan looked under the cub's neck and studied the dark green wavy lines painted across the brown bead.

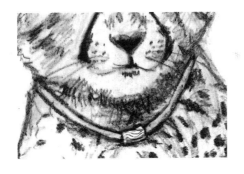

"The wavy green lines remind me of grass blowing in the wind," Nathan said. "How about *Blade*? You know...like for a blade of grass."

"That's a great name," Cassidy said.

Dorian sat up. "Hey, Nathan, this isn't the first time you've done this. Is it?"

Nathan shook his head. "Nope. I used to do this all the time with my best friend, Bobby."

"Wait a minute!" David said. "Why didn't anyone tell us about the secret before?"

"It doesn't work until you're nine. Not sure why," Nathan admitted. "Since Gabby just turned nine, Mom and Dad wanted to wait so you could experience the secret together."

"That's so sweet," Gabby said as she smiled at David. "Aren't you glad you waited for me?"

David looked at Nathan. "Do I really have to answer that question?"

Gabby frowned. "Hmmf."

Just then, Cassidy realized something. "Nathan! So this is why we had to be in the lion's den. You didn't want anyone to see the cubs. Right?"

"Actually, I just thought it would be easier to keep the cubs in one spot," Nathan said. "But do you guys want to know the best part of the secret?"

The kids replied all at once...

"Oh yeah!"

"Tell us!"

"What is it?"

Nathan grinned. "You can play with them in the park."

"*What*?!" David cried. "Are you crazy? What are we supposed to tell everyone?"

"Nothing," Nathan said calmly.

Gabby hugged her cheetah a bit tighter. "But don't you think everyone will ask where the cubs came from?"

"Nope." Nathan smiled. "Because *you* guys are the only ones that can see them."

Everyone gasped.

Nathan leaned back and rested on his elbows with a huge grin. "Told you it was an amazing secret."

Cubs and Candy

"Nathan, is that really true?" Dorian asked.

"Yep."

"Why can't anyone else see them?" Gabby asked.

"Because these beads belong to *our* family," Nathan told her. "Only family and people you choose to share the gift with can see them. And we chose Dorian and Cassidy, remember?"

By now, Blade and Chase had started exploring the den. The two cubs found the boys' backpacks and began chewing on the pockets.

Cassidy noticed the cubs. "Uh...guys, you might want to make sure the cubs don't take anything out of your backpacks."

"They're just exploring," David said. "It's what cubs do. They're fine."

"Don't worry, Cass," Dorian agreed. "It's not like their paws can open zippers." Dorian turned his attention back to Nathan. "So Nathan, you're saying that absolutely no one can see the cubs except us."

Nathan nodded again. "Yep."

Dorian shook his head. "That's just not possible. This just can't be re—"

"Big D," David warned. "If you say this isn't real one more time, I'm gonna put Chase on top of your head!"

"Trust me, Big D," Nathan said. "These cubs are very real."

Sunshine saw the cubs and decided to join them. The two male cubs kept chewing on the side pocket of Dorian's backpack.

Nathan stood up and grabbed his duffle bag. "By the way, when you go outside and play with the cubs, you're gonna have to take pretending to a whole new level."

"What do you mean?" Dorian asked.

"Think about it," Nathan explained. "You're going to be playing with an animal that no one else can see except you. It might look a little weird to the other kids."

"Nathan," David cried. "You can't just leave us!"

"Don't worry," Nathan said. "I'll come back and check on you. Besides, I have to help Coach Tim with Little Dribblers."

Nathan noticed the worried looks on the kids' faces. "Guys, relax! Just have fun with the cubs. But make sure you watch them. Don't let them run off."

Gabby walked toward the wide open door of the lion's den and looked out. She spotted Madison and her gang walking under the metal monkey bars. Even though Gabby wanted to enjoy her new cub, she knew she wasn't ready to face the big bully again. She wrapped her arms around herself and sighed.

Nathan joined Gabby and saw Madison, too. He placed his hands on her shoulders. "It'll be okay, Gabbs. Remember, Sis. Anything is possible." He turned and waved to the rest of the kids. "Have fun, kiddos!" Then Nathan was gone.

Cassidy spoke first. "Well, now what?"

David answered. "I think we should take the cubs outside. They'll get bored in here and that's not fair to them. Cubs like to run and jump and climb trees."

Dorian nodded. "I agree. Let's test this magical stuff outside." He turned to get his backpack and saw Chase licking his lips. "Uh-oh!"

David frowned. "What do you mean 'uh-oh'?"

Dorian looked down and found a red bag of candy right next to Chase's paw. "I think he just ate my Merry Berrys.

The kids looked down at Chase and found small bits of Dorian's chewy peanut butter flavored candy. Oval shaped candies in blue, red, green, and orange colors were scattered underneath Chase's tummy and around his paws.

"Are you sure he ate them?" David asked.

"Look at his tongue," Dorian said. He pointed to Chase, who was still licking his lips. Blue, orange, and green colors stained the cub's long grainy tongue.

"I thought they couldn't get into your backpack, Big D," Cassidy said.

"Oops," Dorian said, feeling a bit guilty.

A sad whimpering sound escaped Chase's lips. He continued to moan as he slowly walked back and forth near the metal wall of the lion's den.

54

"Aww...poor little guy," Gabby said. "He doesn't look like he feels so good. Why is he walking around like that? Is he looking for something?"

David watched the poor cheetah cub searching near the edge of the den. "I know what he's looking for," he said. "and it's not gonna be good."

Now the girls were curious.

Dorian guessed it too. "Yeah, I know exactly what he's looking for."

"*What*?!" the girls cried.

David looked up. "He's probably looking for a place to poop."

The girls gasped. Gabby loved her animals more than anything. The poop—not so much.

"Chase can't go poop in here!" Cassidy cried. "This whole place will be stinky."

"Actually, most wild animals don't leave poop," Dorian said. "They leave scat."

"Yeah," David agreed. "My Grandpa told me that the people at the Cheetah Conservation Fund in Namibia check the scat to see where the cheetahs have been hunting."

"They also use the scat to see if the cheetahs are healthy," Dorian added. "So technically it's not called poop."

"Oh, really." Cassidy raised her eyebrows. "So does that mean that *technically* it won't stink?"

"Uh…we never said that," David replied.

"Then," Cassidy said, "we'd better get him out of here!"

David picked up Chase, who was still moaning. "That's okay, little guy. I'll find a poop spot for you."

Blade and Sunshine couldn't understand why Chase was being picked up. The playful cubs started to whine.

"Hey, I didn't know cheetahs made sounds like that," Cassidy said.

"They make lots of sounds," David told Cassidy. "Most people think they roar like lions, but they don't. They can purr, hiss, mew, and even growl."

"And," Dorian said, "they even call out to each other. It almost sounds like a bird chirping. Kind of like the sound they're making now."

Gabby stood near the entrance of the den, listening to her friends. She realized it was time to get the cubs out. She'd also promised Lucy that she'd read to her today and show her the zebra her nana had sent. She walked back and took the plush animal out of her backpack.

Sunshine immediately saw the toy zebra and wanted it. The sweet cub trotted over and tried to sneak up on the striped animal.

"No, no, Sunshine," Gabby said as she knelt down to pet her cub. "This isn't a toy for you. But I bet we can find you a cool chew toy outside."

The cub stared at her new curly-haired friend and whined again.

She'd be a whole lot happier if she could just get her paws on that zebra. She was so close!

"Okay, guys," David said, "this is the plan. Big D and I will take Chase and Blade to the far end of the park so Chase can go poop. We'll meet you back at the sandbox in ten minutes. Got it?"

"Got it!" the girls replied.

The kids walked out of the lion's den into the warm sunshine and felt the cool ocean breeze nearby. Wild Animal Kids with their magical wild animals.

Together, they went into Safari Park with a secret and the most beautiful gift they could ever have imagined.

Their journey had just begun.

I'm the Great Pretender

The kids stood just outside the wide open door of the lion's den. The park was filled with parents sitting on folding chairs and children scattered around the playground. The Wild Animal Kids didn't know what to expect, so they all just stood there, waiting. Waiting for someone to see the cheetahs.

A few boys ran by chasing each other. "Hey, guys," one of the boys shouted.

"Uh...hey," the kids replied.

The boys, chasing each other in a game of tag, kept on running.

Cassidy grinned. "Wow. The cheetahs really *are* invisible!"

Chase moaned again.

"C'mon, Big D," David said. "We need to get Chase to a poop spot."

As the boys took off, Sunshine jumped out of Cassidy's arms and ran straight for the safari sandbox. Lucy was there with her two-year-old brother, Tommy.

The girls sprinted and followed Sunshine. Even though Sunshine was invisible, they still needed to stay close by to keep an eye on her.

Meanwhile, David and Dorian took their cubs out to the large grassy field by crocodile pond. There weren't really crocodiles in the pond. Huge green statues shaped like Nile crocodiles sat on the edge of the water.

Normally, the pond was filled with kids jumping on the backs of the green crocodiles, but it was almost time for the Striker girls to practice. No one came back here when Madison and her team played soccer.

David set Chase gently on the ground. "There you go, little buddy. Go poop…I mean…go leave your scat wherever you want."

Blade leaped out of Dorian's arms and explored the bushes nearby. He lowered his nose, sniffing the ground as he walked back and forth.

"So, Big D," David said, "since no one can see the cheetahs, do you think they can see the scat?"

Dorian shrugged. "Don't know. Why?"

"Because, if the scat is invisible, then we don't have to clean it up. Right?"

Dorian's eyes lit up. "Hey, you're right! But how do we find out for sure?"

Just then, Chase stopped to poop. It took awhile, but once he was done, he felt a whole lot better.

"Whoa!" David said, covering his nose with both hands. "That has got to be the stinkiest poop in like...the whole wide universe."

Dorian covered his nose too. "You mean scat."

"When it smells that bad, who cares what you call it!"

Chase, who was back to his spunky self, chased Blade. The cubs jumped all over each other until Blade ended up on the ground. But Blade was not about to put up with that.

Blade quickly rolled over and threw Chase off balance. Chase didn't even see it coming. Then Blade sprang up and pounced on top of his cheetah buddy.

Dorian picked up a small twig and went over to Chase's scat.

"Dude!" David cried. "What are you doing? You're not gonna touch it, are you?"

"Davy, I think the reason Chase's scat smells so bad is because of what he ate," Dorian said. "We should examine it. You know…just like how scientists study wild animals in their natural habitats."

"I…guess we can," David said slowly.

David could think of a bunch of cool things he'd like to do as a wildlife scientist. But checking the poop wasn't at the top of his list.

Dorian took the twig and poked it into the smelly scat. "Look at all the colors in Chase's scat," Dorian said. "There's blue…red…green…and even orange colors in here."

"Hey," David said, "those are the colors of your Merry Berry candies."

The boys looked at each other and both shouted, "Grooooss!"

"Let's go, Strikers!" It was Madison. She and her teammates were heading straight for the boys.

"Uh-oh," Dorian said. "What do we do with the scat?"

"Better hope it's invisible," David said, "because they're almost here. Hurry, let's get the cubs."

The boys tried to scoop up the cubs, but the cheetahs didn't want to get picked up. It was playtime! Chase jumped up, tackled Dorian to the ground, and stood on his stomach.

"Seriously!" Dorian cried. "What is it with this cub and my stomach?"

Madison walked up with a few of her teammates following behind. She scowled at the boys. "What kind of stupid game are you two morons playing way out here?"

"We're playing with two cheetah cubs. What do you care?" David shot back.

"Davy!" Dorian cried, "What are you doing? It's suppose to be a secret." He tried to get up, but Chase started licking his face.

"Don't worry, Big D. Madison's too dumb to know that a cheetah cub is right next to her leg."

Madison whipped around and saw...nothing!

"Ha! Made ya look!" David shouted.

Madison really didn't see anything, but Blade was definitely sniffing her leg. Her lotion even made him sneeze.

Madison glared at David. "Figures. You're just another dumb animal nerd, just like your puny sister."

Now David was mad. "If you ever bully my sister again, I'll—"

But before David could finish his warning, a black Labrador puppy came racing through the park. She stopped right in front of Chase and started barking.

Chase hopped off Dorian's stomach and started frolicking with the small pup. Blade ran up and joined them—cats and dog playing with each other right next to Dorian.

Dorian sat up. "David! The puppy can see the cubs."

Madison put her hands on her hips. "Now your stupid pretending game is getting annoying. The puppy just wants to play with you, nerd-brain."

"LADY! LADY! Come here, girl!" It was the Labrador's owner.

The puppy stopped playing with the cubs and looked back. Her owner was running toward her with a purple leash in her hand.

The Labrador barked at the cubs and started jumping all around them. Then, the runaway puppy darted off toward the large bushes by the drinking fountain. The young pup still wanted to play and running was the only way to escape her owner's leash.

The cubs looked up at the boys, wondering what to do next. Then Chase decided to follow the Labrador puppy. Blade was close behind. Together, the cubs sprinted across the grassy field to find their new playmate.

"Davy, we have to go after them!" Dorian looked out and saw the cubs chasing the pup behind a large bush.

Blade actually stopped and looked back at Dorian. It was almost as if the cub was waiting for the boys to follow them.

"You scared off the poor puppy," Madison said. "You need to leave *now*. We're getting ready to practice." Madison turned to her teammates. "C'mon, girls. Let's leave this animal freak show."

Madison flipped her long blonde hair as she walked by David and almost hit him in the face. "Later...Turd Face!"

David glared at the big bully and whispered to himself, "We'll see who's a *turd face*."

Madison didn't know it, but she was walking right up to Chase's scat.

Dorian pulled on David's arm. "Let's go!"

"Ew!" Madison screamed. "There's poop all over my cleats!"

Dorian whispered to David, "I guess the scat isn't invisible."

"Oh! This is so gross!" Madison wailed. She turned and saw David smiling. "David Cedillo! You knew this poop was here, didn't you?"

Dorian nudged David. "C'mon. I know where the cubs went."

David waved to Madison and yelled as he ran off. "See ya, SCAT FACE!"

Madison yelled after him, "What does that even mean?"

David laughed out loud and took off.

The boys ran to look for the cubs in the bushes behind the drinking fountain.

Dorian got there first. "Uh-oh!"

David was right behind him, still smiling. *Scat Face. That's a good one,* he thought.

But as he turned the corner, he saw what Dorian saw.

He wasn't smiling anymore.

I'm Still the Great Pretender

While the boys chased their cheetahs, Gabby and Lucy were reading a book about cheetah cubs. The two girls sat next to each other at the edge of the safari sandbox.

Lucy closed the cheetah book. "Thanks for reading with me, Gabby. The cubs were so cute."

The two girls looked up when they heard Cassidy. Cassidy was chasing Tommy back and forth across the soft sand in the safari sandbox. She growled and jumped around, pretending to be a wild animal.

Lucy couldn't actually see the invisible cub, but Sunshine was running right next to her baby brother.

Lucy grinned. "My brother likes when you chase him, Cass." Even though Lucy was just five, she loved being Tommy's big sister.

Cassidy stopped and looked up, her long red hair covering most of her face with just a few freckles showing. "He's such a cutie pie," she said. "I wish I had a little brother instead of two boring older sisters."

A few strands of Lucy's dark brown hair fell across her face. Gabby reached over and pulled Lucy's hair back behind her ears so she could see Lucy's sparkling brown eyes. Lucy didn't mind at all. She adored Gabby.

Lucy glanced at the pictures on the front of the book. "I bet all cheetah cubs like to play a lot, huh?" Lucy said.

Gabby glanced back at Cassidy, rolling around in the sand with Tommy and Sunshine. The cheetah cub ran around the small toddler and jumped on Cassidy.

Gabby nodded and smiled. "Lucy, I bet you're right."

Lucy picked up the plush zebra sitting next to Gabby's leg. "Heard about Madison. Sorry."

Gabby frowned. "You heard about that?"

Lucy nodded. "Everybody did."

"Everybody?" Gabby could feel her cheeks getting warm. How embarrassing. "Lucy, how did everyone find out?"

"Madison. She always tells when she's been super mean." Lucy quickly looked away.

"Has Madison ever been mean to you?" Gabby asked gently.

Lucy sighed and nodded. "Yeah. One time. When I was playing by the pond with my zebras. She got mad."

"What did she do?" Gabby asked.

"She threw my baby zebra in the pond."

Gabby gasped. "Lucy, that's awful!"

"It's okay," Lucy said sadly. "I had lots of them."

"But Lucy, that was mean," Gabby said. "And it's not fair that the Strikers get to practice soccer by the pond all day."

Cassidy joined the girls. She'd heard everything. "You're right, Gabbs," she said. "It's not fair. By the time the Strikers are done practicing, it's too late and we all have to go home."

Lucy shrugged. "So what do we do?"

Gabby thought for second. Someone had to stop Madison. It just wasn't right.

While the girls talked, Sunshine followed Tommy to his large dump truck sitting in the corner of the sandbox. The toddler plopped down and picked up a red plastic cup. He scooped up the soft sand and poured it into the back of the truck. Tommy flipped a switch and the big dump truck made a loud beeping noise.

Sunshine leaped out of the sandbox and growled. She slowly peeked back in, wondering if her tiny human was safe.

The dump truck lifted its back trailer and sand went flying everywhere. Tommy filled the truck with sand again and pushed the switch. More sand shot out into the air.

Sunshine figured out the game. The tiny human made sand fly and it was her job to catch it. The cub jumped back into the sandbox and began pouncing on the flying sand.

Gabby and Cassidy watched the toddler and cub with their new game.

"My brother loves that truck," Lucy said. "Boys, huh?"

Cassidy and Gabby stole a quick glance, both thinking the same thing. Today, boys weren't the *only* ones who loved dump trucks.

"Hey, you know what?" Lucy said. "My mom told me that cheetahs were in trouble."

"She's right," Cassidy said. "They could even be extinct—all gone—one day. About a hundred years ago, there were almost a hundred thousand cheetahs in the world."

"I didn't know that," Lucy said.

"Now there's only about ten thousand of them," Gabby said.

"Wow," Lucy whispered. "What if they're all gone when I go to Africa?"

"You're going to Africa?" Cassidy asked, shocked.

"Not now, silly" Lucy giggled. "When I grow up. I'm gonna travel to—"

"Gotcha!" Dorian cried.

Dorian landed on the ground right in front of the sandbox. He'd been chasing Chase and had finally caught the speedy cheetah.

The girls frowned and stared at Dorian laying flat on the grass. Only Gabby and Cassidy knew what had just happened. Lucy couldn't understand why Dorian had thrown himself to the ground.

"Wait up!" David called as he ran toward the sandbox. When he got there, David went down on his knees and then fell back on the grass. He was breathing hard and could barely speak.

Chase saw Sunshine playing in the sand with Tommy. The cheetah cub wiggled out of Dorian's arms and pranced right into the sandbox to join the small toddler and Sunshine.

"Uh, Dorian?" Lucy said. "How come you said 'gotcha?' What were you and David chasing?"

Dorian tried to think of something quick. "Um, um…we were chasing each other?"

"How come?" Lucy asked.

David sat up, finally catching his breath. "We were pretending." He nudged Dorian. "Right Big D? We were pre-ten-ding. Remember, genius?" He nudged his best friend again, hoping that Dorian would finally catch on.

"Oh, yeah…yeah!" Dorian grinned. "We were chasing a cheetah."

David nudged Dorian again. This time it was almost a good shove.

Dorian shook his head. "I mean...we were *pretending* to chase a cheetah."

David nodded. "I was the cheetah and Dorian was the predator," he said, speaking to Lucy. "You know, the animals that hunt other animals."

Lucy rolled her eyes. "I know what a predator is. Duh!"

"Uh, Davy," Dorian said. "Just to be clear. I was the cheetah and you were the predator."

David frowned. "How come you get to be the cheetah?"

"Because I got here first," Dorian said. "Which means you were chasing me—the cheetah! Remember? The fastest land animal on the planet!"

David frowned. "Maybe instead of being a predator, you were the prey. Like a Thomson gazelle and I was just about to eat you!"

"Well, if I was the gazelle," Dorian shouted, "then you were the slowest cheetah butt in Africa because you were way...way behind me!"

"Was not!" David shouted back.

"Ahem!" Cassidy interrupted.

The boys turned and faced the girls.

Lucy smiled, staring at the two boys. She liked to pretend too, but these guys were really good at it.

Even the cubs had stopped playing and looked up to see what all the yelling was about.

"We, uh, take our pretending pretty seriously," Dorian said.

Lucy nodded slowly. "Wow…you guys are *really* good pretenders."

In that moment, David remembered something. "Gabbs, I need to talk to you."

"Uh, okay," Gabby said.

David got up and pulled his sister away from the sandbox.

"I'll be right back," Gabby shouted as she and David ran off. "David, what's wrong?"

"Sis, who do you see in the sandbox?"

Gabby glanced back at the safari sandbox. "I see the kids and the cubs. Why?"

"Look again," David said.

Gabby did. Then she gasped. "Oh my gosh, David. There's only two cubs."

Gabby quickly looked back at the cubs' beads. "There's Sunshine, Chase and…oh no. David, where's Blade? Where's Nathan's cub?"

David took a huge deep breath and sighed sadly. "Gabbs…he's lost!"

Chasing Chase

Gabby eyes shot wide open. She was stunned. "David, what happened?"

"Dorian and I took Chase to the edge of the park. He had the worst stomach ache ever."

"How do you know?"

"Because when Chase pooped, it was the stinkiest scat I've ever smelled!" David said. "And then Dorian inspected it. It was actually kinda cool. The scat was mushy and it had all the colors of—"

"DAVID!" Gabby shouted.

"What!"

"I don't want to hear about the poop...or the scat. Get back to what happened."

"Well first, a Labrador puppy wanted to play with the cubs," David replied. "Then Madison stepped in the scat."

Gabby gasped. "She did? Was she mad?"

"Big time! Anyway, the cubs ran off with the puppy. When we found Chase, Blade was gone."

"I didn't know other animals could see our cubs," Gabby said.

"Oh yeah, they can," David replied. "But Nathan totally forgot to tell us about that."

"David! David!" It was Dorian.

Dorian was chasing Chase. Chase was chasing a tall black poodle. The tall black poodle was chasing a fat calico cat. The fat calico cat was chasing a tiny brown squirrel. And the tiny brown squirrel was running for his life!

"Oh, no," David groaned. "Not again. Gotta run!"

The boys found Chase and the other animals at the large oak tree near the dog park. The squirrel was sitting on one of the tallest branches, while the cat had settled for a smaller, unsteady branch. The poodle jumped up on the tree trunk, barking at them to come down.

Chase decided to join the calico cat and tiny squirrel. As the small cheetah climbed up, he came face to face with the chubby cat. The cat growled and hissed at her unwelcomed guest. Chase quickly climbed down and rested on the lowest branch.

"Chase, get down here!" David called.

"Hi, boys." It was Ms. Jessica, Madison's mom. She had just returned from her daily jog around the park. "Did one of you get a new dog?"

David shook his head. "Nope. We don't know who he belongs to."

Ms. Jessica squinted. "It looks like his collar has a tag." She took a dog biscuit out of her pocket and knelt down. "Here boy, come get a treat!"

"Um, Ms. Jessica, do you always have dog treats in your pockets?" David asked.

Ms. Jessica laughed. "Not always, David. But when I run, I never know when I'm going to meet an unfriendly dog. These treats are chicken flavored and dogs love them."

The chicken smell wandered all the way to Chase's cute little black nose. Dogs weren't the *only* ones who loved chicken. Chase sniffed around and spotted the nice lady with the yummy treat in her hand. Surely, it was for him.

The cheetah jumped off the tree and slowly crept up to Ms. Jessica.

Dorian nudged David. They had to do something. If Chase gobbled that dog treat, it would be poopsville all over again.

Chase crouched down and waited for the right moment to steal his treasure. The chicken scent was creeping into his nostrils. He could barely stand it. Chase sprung, ready to claim his prize, but Ms. Jessica stood up before he could snatch the treat. He missed it!

Ms. Jessica called out to the poodle again. "Here, boy. Come get the treat."

The tall black poodle glanced back at the nice lady and then looked up into the tree. He decided that a chicken flavored biscuit was a much better choice than a grumpy fat cat. The dog scampered back to Ms. Jessica and snatched the treat for himself.

Ms. Jessica grabbed the dog's collar. "Look, boys. The tag has a phone number." She pulled out her cell phone and called the owner.

Chase, annoyed with the overgrown puff ball, shook his head and growled at the poodle. As he searched for another treat, the cub spied two chew toys on the nice lady's feet. Bright yellow shoelaces!

Chase yanked and chewed the long, thick strings on her right shoe. Ms. Jessica didn't even notice. She was too busy holding on to the poodle and speaking to the owner on the cell phone.

Dorian shoved David again.

"Will you quit that?" David hissed.

"Do something!"

"Me? Why don't you do something?"

Dorian sighed. "Fine!"

Dorian snuck behind Chase as the cub spit out the wet, yellow shoelace. The cheetah was ready for shoelace number two. But Ms. Jessica started walking toward the dog park just as the cub stood up.

"Oh, yes, I see you now," she said as she spoke into her cell phone. The poodle saw his owner too and started barking.

Dorian lunged for Chase just as the cub tried to run after the other shoelace. Dorian tripped and barely caught the cheetah's hind legs.

Ms. Jessica whipped around. "Oh my goodness, Dorian, are you okay?"

"Um, yeah. I'm okay. I just tripped."

"Are you sure?" she asked. "Maybe I should check your—"

But before Dorian could answer, the black poodle started barking again. The dog jumped and tried to pull away. Ms. Jessica could barely hold on to him.

Chase tugged and pulled, trying to get away too. Then Chase's stomach rumbled and gurgled.

Oh, no! Dorian thought. *Please, please, don't poop. Not now.* But Chase didn't need to poop this time. He just needed to pass some gas—right in Dorian's face.

"Ugh, you have *got* to be kidding me!" Dorian cried. He tried to turn his face away from the gassy smell, but it was no use.

"Okay, boys, I'm going to take the dog back to his owner," Ms. Jessica said.

As she started to leave, David stopped her. "Ms. Jessica, your shoelace is untied."

"Thanks, David. Do you mind holding the dog?" She bent down. "Yuck! My shoelace is all wet and sticky. I must have stepped into a puddle or something."

David just smiled. It was *something* all right.

Ms. Jessica finished tying the wet, slimy shoelace and then took the poodle back to his owner.

David turned to Dorian. "Big D! Are you okay?"

Dorian frowned. "NO! Does it look like I'm okay?"

Chase tried to pull his legs free from Dorian's hands, still trying to escape.

Dorian sat up and pulled Chase close to him. "Here, will you please hold this farting cheetah so I can get up?"

As David bent down to pick up Chase, he saw Blade running. "Hey, there's Blade!"

Chase saw Blade too. The cub wiggled out of Dorian's grip and sprinted off after his cheetah buddy.

"David!" Dorian cried. "You were suppose to hold Chase."

"Sorry. I got distracted when I saw Blade. But look, they're running in the same direction. That's good, right?"

Dorian turned to see where the cubs were heading and shook his head. "David, look. They're running right toward crocodile pond. That's Madison's territory and the Strikers are already practicing. That's not good at all."

David watched the cubs chasing each other and noticed someone running after them. "Hey, there's Nathan."

Nathan had left the basketball courts to check on the kids when he saw the two cubs running. He waved to the boys and shouted, "C'mon, guys!"

The boys started to run after Nathan, but then David quickly stopped.

"What is it?" Dorian asked.

"Dude, you stink!"

"You try putting your face behind a magical cheetah's farting butt," Dorian said. "Then see how good you smell."

David just laughed. "C'mon. Let's go rescue our cubs."

Inside Striker Territory

Gabby picked up her plush zebra and scooped up Sunshine. Together, she and Cassidy left the sandbox in search of the boys. As they headed toward the large oak tree, Chase and Blade sped right by them. A few seconds later, they saw the boys chasing the cubs.

Nathan was in the lead, then Dorian followed.

David was close behind. He saw the girls and shouted, "C'mon!"

"I thought Nathan was playing basketball," Cassidy said.

Gabby shrugged. "I thought he was too." Gabby set Sunshine down on the ground. "We should follow them. Let's go, Sunshine."

Cassidy stopped and pointed. "Look. The cubs are running toward Striker territory. We'd better hurry!"

The girls raced after the boys and found them standing next to each other near a large bush. They were staring out at the field next to crocodile pond.

"What are you guys looking at?" Gabby asked.

The boys didn't answer. They all just pointed.

Madison and her teammates were practicing their passing shots. One girl kicked the ball and almost hit poor Chase in the head. He darted away at the last second.

Another girl almost hit Blade in the stomach. The first ball missed him, but the terrified cub tripped and went tumbling over another soccer ball.

Blade got scared and bolted toward the soccer goal. But as soon as the cub was inside, he realized he was trapped. The frightened little cheetah tried to hide in the right corner of the net.

The Strikers picked up their balls and lined them up in front of the goal. Madison placed her ball in the middle of the line. She always went first.

Blade began chirping loudly, calling for help. The cheetah cub didn't understand what was happening, but he could sense that something was wrong. And he was right.

The Strikers were getting ready to practice their penalty shots. And in the next few moments the girls were going to kick all the soccer balls straight at Blade!

"Oh no," Nathan whispered. "Not again." Nathan sprinted off at lightning speed to save the cub.

"Guys!" Dorian cried. "If Nathan doesn't get there in time, Blade could get hurt. C'mon, let's go help."

"Madison isn't gonna like us going in there," Cassidy said. "She can get really mean."

Gabby stayed silent. She gazed out and watched Madison as she lined up her soccer ball in front of the goal.

She looked down at the plush zebra she was holding and remembered that awful day again. *'Aww...look how cute, ladies. The animal geek still likes to play with her little stuffed ani—'*

"Gabbs," Cassidy said. "Are you listening?"

"Wh...what?" Gabby stammered.

"Gabbs," Cassidy cried, "What's wrong?"

David knew exactly what was wrong. "It's okay, Sis. You stay here with Sunshine. You don't have to deal with Madison again. We've got this."

Gabby nodded slowly, agreeing with her brother. "Um...okay, I'll stay here." But in her heart, she knew it really wasn't okay. It wasn't okay at all. Gabby picked up Sunshine, wrapping her arms around the furry cub.

The cub looked up, sensing the sadness in her curly-haired friend. Then Sunshine reached up and licked Gabby's cheek. Gabby smiled at her cheetah and wondered if Sunshine realized just how much she'd needed that cheetah kiss.

David touched her arm. "We're going in, Sis. We have to help Nathan."

Gabby looked out at the field and stared at Madison again. It wasn't fair that one person could make life so miserable for so many kids. *So many kids*, she thought. Then it came to her. A plan. A plan to confront Madison...once and for all.

Gabby gave Sunshine to Cassidy. "You guys go. I need to go do something. I'll be right back." Gabby dashed off in the opposite direction.

"What was that all about?" Cassidy asked.

David sighed. "I think she's just scared. C'mon, let's go help Nathan."

Nathan's long legs ran faster than they'd ever run in his entire life. His heart was beating so fast he could almost feel it pumping against his shirt.

Blade might be invisible, but that didn't mean the cheetah cub couldn't get hurt. Nathan ran faster. *Please...please! Let me get there in time.*

Blade was still trying to hide. The cub saw the girls getting closer and crouched down even lower.

Chase, on the other hand, was *mad*. He walked around the girls and snuck up on the evil rolling predators.

The balls were still and all lined up. One of the annoying balls had actually hit his butt. Chase crouched down and pounced on the ball bully.

But the dumb ball wouldn't stay still. He rolled right over it! He got up and crouched down again for his next attack, but then he heard Blade calling out for him. Chase growled at the evil ball and then trotted back into the soccer goal with Blade.

"Ugh!" Madison glared at the girl who'd just lost her ball to the invisible cheetah. "Don't you know how to hold on to your ball? Geez!"

The young girl didn't understand why her soccer ball had rolled out of line. It wasn't even a windy day. She walked up and quickly put her ball back in place.

Madison shouted, "I go first!" She backed up, ran, and kicked the ball.

It was going straight for Blade and Chase.

But before the ball flew into the net, Nathan came from out of nowhere. He dove into the air and blocked the flying ball with his body. The ball bounced off his stomach as he hit the ground with a thump.

"Nathan!" Madison cried. "What are *you* doing here?"

Cassidy and the boys ran up. They had seen everything. Nathan had saved Blade and Chase. The kids joined Nathan in front of the net.

As soon as Sunshine saw the cubs she jumped out of Cassidy's arms and ran to join them. She didn't understand what was happening, but she was smart enough to sense danger.

"Now what?" Madison scowled. "What are *they* doing here? You're blocking our goal. You need to leave!"

David looked up at Nathan and whispered, "We can't leave the cubs."

"Don't worry," Nathan whispered back. He glared at Madison and shouted, "We're *not* leaving!"

Madison glared back. She could see the kids whispering to each other. They were definitely up to something. "Fine! Stay. See if I care."

One of the Strikers walked up to Madison. "Maddy, what do we do?"

Madison walked back to her soccer ball and shouted, "Girls, it's time to practice your penalty shots. Everyone kick your balls when I count to three!"

Nathan and the kids gasped.

Madison smiled. This was *her* territory and they were intruders. And on the count of three, she was about to show them who was boss of crocodile pond.

Wildlife Heroes

"Guys!" Nathan cried. "You need to leave or you're gonna get hurt."

"No way, big brother," David said. "Wild Animal Kids stick together!"

Dorian stood up tall and folded his arms. "That's right. Nobody hurts the cubs on our watch!"

Cassidy glared at Madison and shouted, "Bring it on, big bully!" Cassidy bent over with her arms spread out wide. She was ready to block anything that came her way.

Madison shot Cassidy a nasty smile and then turned to her teammates. "READY!" she shouted. "On the count of three, I want you to kick those balls as hard as you can."

"That's *never* gonna happen," said the voice of one very determined little girl.

It was Gabby.

Gabby walked up with Lucy and a group of fifteen other kids. Most of the kids were under the age of seven, and every child was holding a special animal toy. Each child had been bullied and too frightened to say anything before. But together they were ready to fight back. All the kids walked up and formed a long line in front of the soccer net.

Now Madison was really annoyed. "Oh no! Babies and animal-loving geeks are not allowed to play here when we're practicing." Madison pointed to Nathan. "This is all your fault. Don't you ever get tired of playing hero?"

Nathan glanced back at the cubs.

The cheetahs were huddled close together in the far corner of the net, still scared and confused.

Nathan looked at the kids all standing in front of the goal protecting the young cheetahs. They didn't know it, but today these kids were all real wildlife heroes.

Nathan turned to face Madison. "I'm not the hero. These kids are. They are sick and tired of being bullied and they are finally standing up to you. That's a true hero."

Madison was done listening. "What*ever*! Just take all these brats and leave. They are not allowed back here when we're practicing."

Gabby stepped away from the group. "That's not even a real rule. It's just your dumb rule and it's not fair!"

"So what!" Madison spat back.

David joined his sister. "Well today there's a new rule. We get to play back here too and there's nothing you can do about it."

"Yeah!" Lucy shouted as she stomped her foot down. "We're *not* leaving!"

"That's right!" Cassidy shouted. "Besides, you don't even practice near the pond. But you still get mad when kids want to play there."

"Madison," Nathan said, "this field is *huge*. There's room for everyone to play back here. The kids won't get in your way when you're practicing."

Suddenly, Chase started moaning. He jumped up and ran out of the net. It looked like the cheetah cub was trying to run toward the bushes, but he stopped just a few steps behind Madison.

"Uh-oh," David whispered to Dorian. "Do you think he needs to poop again?"

"I think we're about to find out," Dorian whispered back.

One of the Striker girls left her ball and walked up to Madison. "They're right, Maddy. We do have plenty of room to practice. They won't get in our way."

Madison scowled at the young girl. "*I'm* the team captain and *I* make the rules. Besides, I didn't say you could speak!"

The girl scowled right back. Now she was angry. "Maddy, ever since you became team captain, you've made us all look like bullies." The girl's voice got louder. "You're always trying to impress us because your dad's the coach. But if I have to be a bully to be a Striker, then I quit!"

The girl picked up her soccer ball and joined the kids in front of the net. Then, one by one, all of the Striker girls picked up their soccer balls and formed a line next to the kids.

Madison watched as her teammates grabbed their balls and joined the kids in front of the goal. She shook her head in disbelief. How could they leave her after all she'd done for them. She'd tried to be the best team captain in the league. How could they not understand that? Madison was furious.

Madison just stood there. She and her soccer ball now faced the crowd…all alone.

Nathan folded his arms. Like Dorian had said, no one was going to hurt these cubs today. "What's it gonna be Madison?"

Madison wanted to cry but she was too angry. "Fine! I don't need any of you!" Then everything happened at once...

Madison went to get her ball, but instead of picking it up she got behind it and aimed the soccer ball at Gabby.

Chase pooped right behind her left foot and then quickly scurried away into the bushes next to the fence.

Madison ran and kicked the ball as hard as she could. The soccer ball was heading straight for Gabby.

David saw the ball coming and stood in front of Gabby to protect her. He put his hands up in front of his face, hoping to block the ball.

Nathan lunged in front of both of them and kicked the ball with his left foot just in time. He sent it flying back just as hard as Madison had kicked it.

The ball hit Madison in the middle of her stomach. She flew back and landed right on top of Chase's scat!

Everyone gasped.

Madison looked down, smelling the gross gooey poop and screamed. The bright colored poop was smeared across her silky, green soccer shorts.

At first, everyone was too shocked to move. Then, some of the younger kids started to giggle. A bully sitting in poop didn't look so mean now.

Gabby stared at Madison. Tears streamed down Madison's cheeks as she sobbed and hiccupped. Patches of grass and dirt smeared her legs, and a few strands of her blonde hair stuck to her wet cheeks. The park bully was a mess!

Anything is possible, Gabby thought. Last week, Gabby had been terrified of Madison. She'd embarrassed Gabby and had made her feel ashamed for being an animal lover.

But today, Madison was sitting in poop. Today, it was possible to be just as mean as Madison had been. Only, somehow it didn't feel right. It didn't feel right at all.

Gabby faced the group. "Guys! Don't laugh. She's really upset."

"But, Gabbs," Cassidy cried, "she was trying to hurt you!"

"I know," Gabby said softly. "But I feel bad for her."

Nathan looked down at Gabby and smiled. Only his little sister would find a way to be nice to the park bully in trouble. He wasn't surprised. After all, Gabby didn't have a mean bone in her body.

Gabby sighed. She didn't care what Madison had done. No one deserved to be embarrassed like this.

She pulled on Nathan's shirt and whispered in his ear. "I want to help her. She's sitting in Chase's scat. That's kind of our fault."

"Okay, Sis," Nathan whispered. "Let's take care of the cubs first."

He turned and looked for the cubs. Nathan found the cheetahs sitting close together near the bushes next to the pond.

Chase looked bored, but Blade and Sunshine were still leery of all the kids.

Nathan tapped Cassidy's arm and led her away from the kids. "Cass, you and Dorian stay with the cubs. The cubs are over there. See 'em?"

"Yeah. I've been watching them this whole time." Cassidy walked back and nudged Dorian's arm. Together, they quietly snuck off to look after the cheetahs.

Nathan walked back and noticed Gabby and David whispering to each other. "So, guys, what do you want to do?"

Gabby looked up at her big brother with the most determined look Nathan had ever seen. "It's time to make a deal!"

Then Gabby and David took off and walked straight toward Madison. It was time to confront the bully, once and for all.

Let's Make a Deal

Nathan and all the kids followed Gabby and David as they walked toward Madison.

"Gabby, what are we doing?" Lucy asked.

Gabby turned around and spoke to everyone. "I think we need to give Madison another chance."

"But she's been mean to *all* of us!" Lucy cried.

"I know, but like my dad says, *'Always try to be the better person and do the right thing.'*" Gabby looked back at Madison. "And today, the right thing to do is to help Madison."

Nathan agreed. "My sister's right, Lucy. Just because Madison hasn't been very nice, doesn't mean that any of us have to be the same way."

Lucy tugged on Gabby's arm and whispered, "Can we be mean for just a little bit?"

Gabby gave her five-year-old reading buddy a good stare and whispered back, "No!"

Lucy sighed loudly and crossed her arms. "Fine!"

Madison looked up as the kids came near her. She still had tears rolling down her cheeks. "Are you happy now?" She wiped away her tears and looked away. "I know you're all laughing at me."

"We're not here to laugh at you," Gabby said softly.

"Then why are you here?" Madison didn't trust her.

"We're here to make a deal," Gabby said.

Madison frowned and turned back to see what Gabby was up to. "What kind of a deal?"

David spoke up. "You stop being a bully, and we won't say anything about you sitting in scaa…I mean, poop."

Gabby nodded. "Yeah, it'll be our secret. Because if all of the other kids find out about what happened today, everyone *will* laugh at you."

David took a quick glance to check on the cubs. He couldn't find Chase, but Sunshine and Blade were up in a tree. Dorian was calling the cubs, trying to get the cheetahs to climb down. Cassidy wasn't waiting. She had already started climbing up the tree.

As Cassidy climbed up, Sunshine decided to move up to a taller branch. The frightened cub stared at all the kids near the soccer net, wondering if she should go up a little farther. Blade wasn't sure if it was safe to come down either. Those big round balls had been pretty scary.

The two cubs heard Dorian calling out to them again. Sunshine wasn't moving and as far as Blade was concerned, climbing down was not about to happen anytime soon.

David turned back to Madison. "So what do you think, Madison? Do we have a deal?"

Madison looked at everyone and stayed silent. She still didn't know what to do. How could she trust the kids to keep her secret after she'd been so mean to all of them?

Nathan crouched down next to Madison. "Maddy, I've known you for a long time. This isn't you. What's going on?"

Madison dropped her gaze. "When my dad practices with us on Wednesdays, he never lets any kids play back here."

"Yeah, I know," Nathan said. "Coaches reserve the park for their teams on those days. He's right. Kids aren't allowed on the field during practice."

Madison looked up at Nathan. "On Fridays, he puts me in charge and he told me to do the same thing. He doesn't want little kids back here when we practice."

Nathan frowned. "He can't do that. It's a 'Long Beach Kids' park day. The park has to be open to all of us."

"Wait a minute," David said. "Did your dad *tell* you to be a bully?"

Madison sighed. "He said to…'do whatever it takes.'" Madison's shoulders drooped. "He can get a little intense with his soccer."

"Ya think?" David cried.

One of the Strikers walked up to Madison. "Maddy, we never knew your dad asked you to do that. But Nathan's right. Technically, we have to let kids play back here on Fridays."

Madison knew her teammate was right. She'd actually hated becoming the park bully, but she wanted to make her dad happy.

She could still hear him…*"Madison, if your team loses, it will be your fault. Don't be a weak team captain. Make sure those bratty kids don't bother you when you practice on Fridays."*

But today, Madison was done being a bully. She didn't care what her dad thought. Maybe it was time to talk to her mom.

Madison looked up at Gabby and David. "You promise no one will talk about what happened today?"

Gabby and David both nodded. "We promise," they said.

Madison stood up. The smell was so bad that everyone took a few steps back. Madison covered her nose with the back of her hand to keep from throwing up.

"So do we have a deal?" Gabby asked.

Madison reached out to shake Gabby's hand. "Deal."

"That's okay," Gabby said sweetly. "We don't have to shake. You got a little poop on your hands."

"Ew! This is so disgusting," Madison cried. "Where is all this poop coming from?"

Gabby and her brothers quickly glanced at each other and then faced Madison.

They just shrugged and didn't say a word.

As Madison took off to change out of her stinky shorts, some of the younger kids scattered off to play by the green crocodile rocks.

Nathan walked up to his brother and sister. "You guys were pretty amazing today."

Gabby punched her brother in the arm. "You were pretty amazing yourself."

David held out a closed fist to Nathan. "Thanks for saving the cubs. Those balls could have really hurt them."

Nathan bumped his brother's fist. "No problem. These cubs are fun, but they're a big responsibility."

"Tell me about it," David said. "I've been chasing cheetahs all day!"

"Uh…David," Gabby said as she pointed. "I think you better go chase Chase again."

David turned around and found Chase sitting next to a duffle bag. It belonged to one of the

Strikers. His cub had taken out a sneaker and was chewing on the shoelaces. He looked liked one happy little cheetah.

"Seriously?" David groaned. "What is it with that cheetah and shoelaces?"

"I'm glad those aren't my shoes," Nathan said with a big grin. "Listen, we only have a few hours before we have to leave. I'll meet you at the lion's den before we go home."

Nathan went back to the basketball courts, and David ran to save the sneakers from his cub's sharp teeth.

Before Gabby left, she looked out across the large, grassy field next to crocodile pond. Some of the younger boys were chasing each other on the Nile crocodile rocks. A few of the girls had set up their own safari camp with their small animals near the edge of the pond.

Lucy was sitting on the grass with two girls from the Striker team. She was telling them all about cheetahs as she turned the pages in her *"Cheetah Cubs"* book.

Even Madison had returned with a clean pair of shorts. She was actually showing a young girl how to kick a soccer ball.

Gabby smiled.

It wasn't Striker territory anymore.

Nathan had been right.

Anything is possible…if you just believe.

Lizard Tails and Butterflies

For the next few hours, the kids kept busy with the cubs. At first, the boys and their cheetahs climbed trees together. Then Chase started peeing and marking each tree as his own personal play tree. The last tree Chase decided to pee on was right in front of Ms. Billie's knitting club.

One of the girls stood up and started sniffing the air. "Ms. Billie!" the girl cried. "I smell something. I think someone just went pee-pee!"

David scooped up his peeing cheetah and quickly ran off toward the rhino rocks with Dorian and Blade. Ms. Tammy's preschoolers were nearby on the grass working on their art projects. Thankfully, Chase didn't pee on any of the rocks near the kids.

Blade jumped on the largest rhino rock and found a blue-bellied lizard sunning itself. He tried to grab it, but the lizard was too fast. The only thing Blade caught in his mouth was the tail that the lizard left behind. The cheetah cub jumped down on the grass to play with his new toy.

Chase saw the lizard tail hanging from Blade's mouth and decided he wanted it too. Soon, the two cubs were playing tug of war with the leftover tail. Chase growled and pulled harder. Blade let go, and both lizard tail and Chase went flying backwards, crashing into Ms. Tammy's art supplies.

Crayons, paintbrushes and an open tube of glitter exploded all over the kids. The children jumped up off the grass and started screaming. A few of them tried to shake the glitter off their clothes and out of their hair.

Ms. Tammy searched around for the culprit, but the cubs had already slipped away. Dorian and David chased them to the far end of the park...again!

Meanwhile, the girls followed Sunshine as she chased a single butterfly through a patch of yellow dandelions.

The Monarch Butterfly danced in the wind as she spread her beautiful orange and black wings wide open. She floated from flower to flower, always keeping ahead of Sunshine.

Sunshine, with her heavy, furry paws, pounced on every dandelion the butterfly had visited. Just two beautiful wild creatures playing a game of tag in Safari Park.

Gabby and Cassidy tried to catch the butterfly too, but it was no use. The delicate insect fluttered up, down, and all around them. No one would catch her today.

Finally, the Monarch Butterfly perched herself on one of the flowers. She just sat there, with her straw-like tongue sucking nectar from the dandelion.

Sunshine watched the butterfly as it drank nectar from the bright yellow flower. The silly butterfly didn't appear to be scared at all! Sunshine licked her lips and tried to pounce on the tiny creature one last time. The butterfly, though small, was again too quick for the cheetah cub. It flew away, leaving poor Sunshine without anything to chase.

Cassidy got an idea and dashed off to get two bubble blowers out of her backpack. As the girls blew into their wands, Sunshine and a group of toddlers chased the soapy bubbles. Gabby thought it was the sweetest thing she'd ever seen.

The Wild Animal Kids played with their wild cheetahs cubs for hours. Dorian jotted notes in the club's animal journal, while David sketched the cubs playing in the bushes. As the sun was beginning to set, everyone knew it was time to head back to the lion's den.

Cassidy found Blade sleeping on top of one of the rhino rocks.

When Cassidy called out to him, he just stared at her. Cassidy called again. Nope. He was *not* moving off his cozy, warm rock.

Cassidy finally climbed up and picked up the sleepy cheetah. She had to carry him all the way back to the lion's den.

David gathered up the journal and his sketchpad and headed back to the lion's den first. He wanted to speak to Nathan before the other kids got there.

David searched for Chase and found Dorian trying to catch his little cheetah. Chase was running around the green merry-go-round in circles. The children sitting on top of the merry-go-round were screaming, "Run, Dorian, Run!"

The younger kids actually thought that Dorian was playing with them. They didn't even realize that Dorian was *actually* trying to catch an invisible cheetah cub.

David chuckled at first, wondering if Dorian could catch Chase. Then David frowned. Suddenly, something felt wrong.

For the first time since the cubs had arrived, David felt a deep sadness. And he knew why.

Today, he'd met a magical cheetah.

A cheetah who had changed his life and touched his heart.

A cheetah, whose time at Safari Park had run out.

It was time to say...goodbye.

The First Goodbyes

David stepped into the lion's den and saw his big brother sitting on the ground. Nathan was staring at the beads in the wooden box so intently, that he didn't even hear his little brother.

David thought Nathan looked...sad. "Hey, whatcha doin'?"

Nathan slammed the bead box shut. "Nothing," he said quickly.

David knew something was wrong, but he didn't push. "So, today was just about the most amazing day *ever*!"

Nathan grinned. "It was pretty cool, huh?"

"You did this a lot, didn't you?" David asked as he sat down next to the bead box.

"Yeah, I did...but I stopped using the beads until today," Nathan said softly.

David frowned. How could anyone not want to use the magic of the beads? Hanging out with wild cheetahs had been one of the most incredible experiences of his life.

David looked down at the wooden box filled with the beads that had changed his life forever. He picked it up and traced his finger around the white crystal elephant.

It still seemed impossible. How could a box filled with magical beads bring over wild animals? And how did the box work when they had to send them home? David actually didn't want an answer to his last question, because he wasn't ready for Chase to go home.

David focused on Nathan again. He knew something was bothering his older brother.

"Hey, when you saw Blade stuck in the soccer net, I heard you say, 'not again'," David said. "What did you mean by that?"

Nathan sighed. "It's a long story."

"Will you tell me later?" David asked.

Nathan nodded. "Sure. How about tonight after—"

"Hey, hey!" Cassidy laughed as she stepped into the den with Blade in her arms. "Who wants some furry, fluffy gifts?"

Gabby and Dorian followed close behind with the other two cheetah cubs.

Dorian was trying to hang on to Chase, who was trying to jump off his shoulder. "I don't think this cub ever gets tired!" Dorian gently placed the cub on the ground.

Sunshine, on the other hand, sat sweetly in Gabby's arms, with her small paws resting in Gabby's long curls.

Gabby laughed. "Sunshine loves...loves my hair."

Nathan placed the bead box right in front of him. "C'mon, guys, let's all sit down. Is everyone ready to send the cheetahs back?"

No one said anything, because no one was really ready to say goodbye. Today, they had created a new club just for animal lovers—'The Wild Animal Kids Club'. They all knew that they'd learn about endangered animals. But they never imagined learning with their very own magical, wild creatures.

"I just want to say," Cassidy said, "that today was one of the most amazing and coolest days of my life."

Dorian nodded. "I agree. I didn't believe today was even possible. This secret is pretty awesome."

Nathan grinned. "It is pretty special."

Chase yawned and rubbed his eye with his paw. David's feisty little cub was finally getting tired. Chase walked over and jumped into David's lap. David scratched his cheetah's neck. The tired cub rested his head on David's leg and purred happily.

Nathan glanced out into the park through the lion's open doorway. The park looked empty. Nathan knew it was time to send their cheetah friends home.

He glanced around and noticed the worried looks on all the kids. He sighed, knowing what was coming. The first goodbyes were always the hardest.

"Okay, guys," Nathan said. "The cubs need to sit together before they leave. It's time to say goodbye to your cheetahs. Gabbs, why don't you go first?"

Gabby placed a kiss on top of Sunshine's furry head. "Goodbye, my sweet Sunshine. I'll never forget you." Gabby picked up her cub and placed Sunshine in front of the kids.

Cassidy was holding Blade. "Bye, little guy. No more running into soccer nets, okay?" Cassidy hugged the cub and placed Blade right next to Sunshine.

David was last. He lowered his head next to Chase's face. "Goodbye, little buddy. Today was the best day of my life. I'll miss you." David lifted the sleepy cub and placed him right next to Blade and Sunshine.

The cheetahs sat still, staring at all of the kids. It was almost as if the cubs knew that it was time to say goodbye.

"Now what do we do?" Gabby asked Nathan.

"Since we were all part of the cheetahs' lives today, we need to imagine the cubs going home...somewhere safe."

All the kids closed their eyes and imagined the cubs in a warm, safe, and loving home.

"Okay," Nathan said, "open your eyes and repeat after me." Nathan took a deep breath. "I imagine..."

The kids kept their eyes on the cheetahs and repeated Nathan's magical words, "I imagine..."

"I believe..." Nathan said.

"I believe…" the kids repeated.

"YOU…are…cheetah!" Nathan cried.

"YOU…are…cheetah!" The kids cried.

Within seconds, the cubs' beads glowed brighter and brighter against their furry necks. Rays of light shot out from the beads. The lights swirled and danced in the air until they formed the golden portal.

Sunshine stood up first. She quickly turned and hopped into the magical doorway.

Blade got up and decided to stretch. His front paws clawed the dirt as his rear end lifted up in the air. He opened his mouth and let out a huge yawn, showing off his pink tongue and sharp white teeth. He was ready for another nap. Blade turned and calmly stepped into the portal.

Finally, it was Chase's turn. Instead of heading into the portal, the cheetah cub walked up to David and licked him on the cheek.

Tears pricked the back of David's eyes. "I'll miss you, little buddy." David stroked his cub's face one last time.

Chase purred as he nuzzled his face against David's hand. Then, the cub slowly turned away and headed for the portal. But before he jumped in, Chase turned and chirped, calling out to David.

David thought it was the saddest sound he'd ever heard. He gazed at his cheetah friend, wondering if he'd ever see him again.

Chase finally jumped through the golden, magical portal. The last cheetah cub had gone home.

The lights swirled around faster and faster. With each spin, the golden rays became brighter and brighter.

Suddenly, a thick beam of light burst out of the magical doorway, shooting out the three beads worn by the cheetah cubs.

The swirling portal immediately vanished. The golden rays of light disappeared, leaving behind only one thing. The beads.

The children stared at the magical beads that had belonged to *Sunshine, Blade* and *Chase.* The beads sat still, scattered on the patches of grass in front of them.

The cheetah cubs…were gone.

Chosen

David couldn't believe that Chase was really gone. He didn't remember ever feeling as sad as he felt right now. He grabbed Chase's bead off the ground and wrapped his fingers around it.

Cassidy took her best friend's hand and squeezed it. "You okay?"

Gabby nodded slowly. "She was a cutie, huh?"

"Yeah," Cassidy agreed, "she was pretty sweet."

Dorian sat quietly with his thoughts, going over everything that had happened in one day. He still couldn't believe what he'd just experienced. But he had experienced it. All of it. Running and playing with wild cheetahs in their very own Safari Park.

David wiped a single tear off his cheek. "Nathan, will we ever see them again?"

Nathan reached over and picked up Sunshine's and Blade's beads. "It depends," he said. "Since Dad and Mom are Wildlife Warriors, we get to make a connection with a special animal. An animal that chooses us."

David was confused. "What do you mean...'a connection?'"

"It's when an animal comes into your life and you can't ever imagine your life without that animal. It's almost like they're a part of you," Nathan explained. "Chase walked up and licked you on the face. He even called out to you before he jumped into the portal. I think he chose you."

David thought about his day with Chase. He couldn't imagine his life without Chase. That just felt wrong. David nodded. "Chase did choose me. I can feel it!"

Nathan nodded and agreed. "I think he did too. So take care of Chase's bead. Don't ever...*ever* put it back into the box."

Gabby frowned. "What happens if we put the beads back into the box?"

"When you put the beads back in, the box repaints the beads," Nathan said. "You can never find the same bead again, and every animal is tied to one bead and one bead only."

"How is it possible for a wooden box to paint beads?" Dorian asked Nathan.

Cassidy leaned over and whispered. "Maybe with something called...mmmmagic!"

Nathan grinned. "She's right, Big D." Nathan took the wooden box and placed it in front of him. "Watch this," he said.

Everyone sat still, staring at the magical wooden box, waiting to see what Nathan was about to reveal.

Nathan opened the lid and placed Blade's bead back into the box. As soon as he closed it, a cloudy blue mist covered the bead box. Within a few seconds, the mist faded away.

He lifted the box toward the kids. "See? The box repainted Blade's bead and replaced Chase's bead with a new one."

Dorian stared into the wooden box, looking for Blade's bead. But it wasn't there. "How is that possible?" Dorian asked. "And why did the box replace Chase's bead?"

Nathan brought the box closer to Dorian. "When David decided to keep Chase's bead, the box knew it had to replace it. The box will always end up with ten beads."

Cassidy looked in and counted all the beads. "But, Nathan," she said, "there's only nine beads in the box."

"I know," Nathan replied. "The box is waiting on Gabby to decide if she's going to keep her bead or not."

"Did I connect?" Gabby wondered. "Did Sunshine choose me?"

Nathan gave her Sunshine's bead. "I don't know. You tell me. Are you willing to put Sunshine's bead

124

back into the box? You'll never see her again. How does that make you feel?"

Gabby thought for a moment. "I had a lot of fun with her. And now that she's gone, I feel a little sad," she said. "But not for me...for her. Poor Sunshine won't ever get to come out and play again."

"Actually," Nathan said, "that's not true. Just like the box repaints the beads for us, it does the same thing for other Wildlife Warriors around the world."

"Really?" Gabby asked.

"Oh yeah," Nathan said. "The animals shift and move throughout the portals with lots of kids. And one day, Sunshine and Blade will choose a special person to connect with."

Gabby smiled. "That makes me feel better." Gabby placed her cheetah's bead back into the magical box. The blue mist appeared again and repainted Sunshine's bead.

David took a deep breath as he held Chase's bead even tighter. His bead was *never* going back into that box. "Trust me, Sis. When you're chosen, you'll know it. I've never felt anything like it."

"Just remember," Nathan said, "once the animals choose you, you'll always be responsible for them. You'll always be connected for life."

"Wow," Cassidy whispered. "This is the best secret of my entire life! What animals should we bring in next?"

The kids stood up and started speaking all at once. Cassidy was ready to bring in a baby panda, Dorian was curious about lions, and Gabby thought a tiger cub would be fun. David just wanted to see Chase again.

Gabby picked up the sign that she'd made for their club and looked at it again.

Cassidy walked up and smiled. "That's a cool club sign, girly girl. It came out perfect."

"Almost perfect," Gabby said as she reached into her backpack. "I just got these from my nana."

Gabby took out a small envelope filled with animal sticker stamps and showed them to Cassidy.

"Wow, those are so cool," Cassidy said.

Gabby took the cheetah stamp and stuck it next to David's picture on the Wild Animal Kids Club sign that she'd made. "There...now it's perfect."

"We should put a sticker next to our picture when we bring our favorite animal over," Cassidy said.

Gabby nodded. "Good idea."

Nathan walked to the door of the lion's den. He saw his best friend, Bobby, heading out from the basketball courts. It was time to go home.

"C'mon, guys," Nathan said. "We should go. I told Bobby to meet us in the parking lot." Nathan walked back and slipped the wooden box into his duffle bag.

The kids headed out and saw parents packing their cars with children, folding chairs, and toys. The sun had disappeared into the Pacific Ocean, leaving behind a beautiful bluish-gold sunset.

As the kids left the park, they heard loud screeching sounds. A large flock of Long Beach's bright green parrots squawked as they flew above the huge wooden Safari Park sign.

The kids stopped and watched the graceful parrots fly away. Each child also took one last look at the grand entrance standing in front of them.

Today, the wooden cheetah had a special meaning for all of them.

Today, they would leave Safari Park with a secret.

The secret of the magical beads that opened a mysterious doorway to a world of wild creatures.

It was a secret powered by their imagination and the belief that anything was possible.

It was a gift they would treasure…forever!

Here's a sneak peak from

The Wild Animal Kids Club – Book 2

I...am...Wolf!

Shadow

It was Friday night at the Cedillos and as far as David was concerned, it was the best night of the week. Why? Because it was a sleepover night! Their best friends, Dorian, Cassidy, and Bobby came over every Friday night after a 'Long Beach Kids' park day at Safari Park.

Tonight was extra special. His dad had just returned from a zoo in Texas. He'd been called away to help save a Bengal tiger that needed surgery. Since he was one of the top wildlife surgeons in the country, he traveled a lot.

David and Dorian were researching wildlife conservation groups on the computer when Gabby and Cassidy burst through David's bedroom door.

"Excuse me!" David scowled at his sister. "You did learn how to read, right?"

Gabby rolled her eyes. "Of course I know how to read."

David pointed to his door.

"How many signs do I need to put on my door before you start knocking?" David asked. Gabby always forgot to knock.

Gabby poked her brother on the shoulder. "David, I know you're just joking." She and Cassidy walked right past him, hopped on his bed, and sat on top of his cheetah pillows.

David sighed. It wasn't the first time Gabby just decided to come in when she wanted.

"Do you guys want to help us with the Wild Animal Kids scrapbook?" Gabby asked. "Cassidy and I decorated the cover with some of my stickers."

Cassidy opened a small brown envelope. "Your grandpa and nana sent some great pictures of the cheetahs in Namibia," Cassidy said. She took out a few cheetah photos and showed them to the boys.

David frowned. "You want me to put *these* pictures in *that* book with your girly stickers?" He looked at the two girls like they were crazy. "I would rather have all of my teeth pulled out by Grandpa's dentist. And you know how old Grandpa's dentist is."

Dorian looked up from the computer screen. "Same goes for me."

Gabby just shook her head. "C'mon, Cassidy. These boys don't know how to have any fun."

The girls hopped off the bed and ran back to Gabby's room.

David shut his door. "I told you, Big D. Being an only child is the only way to go. You don't know how lucky you are."

Dorian just smiled and went back to reading David's computer screen. Dorian was reading about 'The Cheetah Conservation Fund' in Namibia where David's grandparents had volunteered.

"Did you find them, Big D?"

Dorian nodded. "Yep. Did you know that Dr. Laurie Marker started a guard dog program to help save the cheetahs?"

"Really?" David asked. "How do dogs help the cheetahs?"

"Since the farmers are using more land, sometimes their livestock can get too close to the cheetahs," Dorian explained. "And you know what that means."

David grinned. "Dinner is served. Cheetahs don't have to run very fast to catch a goat."

Dorian kept reading. "It says here that they breed Anatolian Shepherd and Kangal dogs. They give them to African farmers when they're puppies so they can bond with the herd."

David looked over Dorian's shoulder and read too. "Wow. Pretty smart. The dogs don't hurt the livestock and when they bark, they scare away predators."

Dorian added a few more notes to the Wild Animal Kids Club journal. "This Dr. Laurie Marker is a pretty smart lady," he said. "If the dogs scare the cheetahs away, then the farmers won't have to hurt them anymore."

"Hey guys!" Nathan and his friend, Bobby, walked in—without knocking.

"Seriously!" David cried.

Nathan put his hands up. "Listen. I have something I want to show you. Meet us in the backyard behind the orange trees and bring Chase's bead."

Nathan and Bobby left as quickly as they had come in.

"What was that all about?" Dorian asked. "And why does he want you to bring Chase's bead?"

David felt around for Chase's bead in his pocket. "Who knows? C'mon, let's go find out."

David and Dorian walked past Gabby's bedroom. They could hear the girls singing as they worked on their scrapbook. The boys thought they sounded terrible.

"Do you think they're tone deaf?" Dorian whispered.

David nodded and whispered back. "Definitely. What's worse is when they're both in the car. They sing to everything on the radio!"

Dorian shook his head. "That sounds painful. Nobody's ears should have to listen to that!" Maybe it wasn't so bad to be an only child, Dorian thought.

The boys headed down the hall and slipped out through the back patio door.

Nathan and Bobby were already waiting for them. Bobby had been Nathan's best friend since they were five. He looked like a typical California surfer, with sky-blue eyes and long blond hair that was tied back in a ponytail.

"So what's up?" David asked.

Before Nathan could answer, Gabby and Cassidy opened the sliding glass door and ran up.

"We're here," Gabby said. "What's going on?"

"I have something to show you guys," Nathan said. "But first, I want to give this to David."

Nathan took a brown leather cord with a metal clasp out of his pocket and gave it to David. "Here, put Chase's bead on this. Now you can wear it and always have Chase nearby."

David took the cord. "Cool. Thanks."

Bobby nudged Nathan. "Dude, show them yours."

Nathan reached into the collar of his shirt and pulled out a leather cord with a dark black bead. An image of a full moon was painted in the center of the bead.

"You were chosen, too?" David asked.

Nathan nodded. "Yeah, I was."

"What kind of animal did you connect with?" Gabby asked.

"A gray wolf," Nathan replied. "His name's *Shadow*. I haven't brought him back in awhile. The last time he was with me he got hurt."

"What happened?" Cassidy asked.

"Shadow was only four months old when I brought him back again through the portal," Nathan paused, remembering that horrible day.

The kids sat still, waiting for Nathan to finish.

"I left him for just a second to get him some water," Nathan said. "He walked right in front of the swings and a big kid kicked him in the middle of his stomach."

The kids gasped.

"Poor little wolf," Gabby whispered.

"If it wasn't for Dad," Nathan said, "I don't think he would've survived. We had to nurse him for almost a whole month."

"Wait!" David said. "Where did you keep him?"

"At Grandpa's and Nana's house," Nathan replied. "You and Gabbs were still too young to see animals, so Dad thought it was better to keep Shadow at their house."

"What happened after your wolf got better?" Dorian asked.

Nathan sighed. "I sent him back into the portal and I haven't seen him since." Nathan paused for a second and then spoke. "But after seeing you guys today with your cheetah cubs, I realized something…"

"What did you realize?" Gabby asked.

"I stopped using the beads because I was scared," Nathan said. "Scared that I wouldn't be able to protect Shadow like I should."

David remembered when Chase and Blade had run into the soccer net earlier that day. If the girls had practiced their penalty shots before Nathan had got there, the cubs could have been injured.

"Just because they're invisible doesn't mean they can't get hurt," David said. "Are you ever going to see Shadow again?"

This time, Nathan had a huge grin on his face. "Yep. Right now. You guys want to meet him?"

The kids eyes lit up.

"That would be awesome!" David said.

Nathan unhooked the black leather cord from behind his neck and removed Shadow's bead. He closed his eyes and imagined his wolf prowling through the forest. He opened his eyes and gazed down at the bead. "You guys, ready?"

All the kids nodded.

Nathan spoke. "I choose to share this gift with my family and friends sitting here with me."

Then Nathan blew into the bead and recited the magical words. "I imagine..." He blew again. "I believe..." Then he blew for the last time. "I...am...wolf!"

Nathan placed the bead in front of him. As soon as the bead touched the ground, it shook just slightly. A gold light shot up out of the bead and swirled around until it formed the magical portal.

The kids watched and waited. Suddenly, a grayish-black paw gently stepped out.

Nathan watched and waited, too with a huge grin on his face. It was time to say hello to his old friend.

Shadow took his next step, this time revealing his entire body.

Shadow sniffed around and found Nathan. The big gray wolf slowly walked up to him and licked his face.

Nathan laughed. "Hey, big guy. I've missed you. Look at you! You're all grown up!"

Nathan turned to the kids. "Guys, meet Shadow!"

Real Cheetahs! Real Facts!

Cheetah (Acinonyx jubatus)

Fact 1: Over a hundred years ago, there were almost 100,000 cheetahs in the world. Today there are less than 10,000 cheetahs on the planet. Cheetahs are in trouble and need our help.

Fact 2: Cheetahs are the fastest animals on land and they can reach speeds up to 70 mph (112 kph).

Fact 3: Cheetahs are built for speed with their lean muscular body and flexible spine. Their long tail helps them turn and keep their balance when they are running. The cheetah's *'semi non-retractable claws'* act like cleats, as they dig into the ground to gain better footing when they are running.

Fact 4: Dark tear marks under the cheetah's eyes attract the sunlight, which helps to keep the sun's glare out of their eyes.

Fact 5: Cheetahs have wonderful vision. They can spot prey or predators from as far as 3 (5km) miles away.

Fact 6: Cheetahs are skilled hunters. They catch prey about 50% of the time. They hunt animals mostly during the late morning or early evening.

Fact 7: Cheetahs use large trees to leave their scent in order to mark their territory. These trees are called *'Playtrees'*. Scientists use the trees to study the cheetah's social behaviors.

Fact 8: Cheetahs are carnivores, which means they like to eat meat. They usually prey on smaller antelope, such as the springbok and Thomson gazelle.

Fact 9: A cheetah raises her cubs all by herself. She must protect them and teach them the skills to hunt on their own. The cubs will stay with their mother until they have mastered these skills.

Fact 10: When the cheetahs are full grown, the females will go off and live by themselves. The males will stay together and form their own group, called a coalition.

FACT OR OPINION – It's up to you!
But as far as David is concerned...
"Cheetahs are the coolest animals on the planet!!"

Wildlife Hero Spotlight

Dr. Laurie Marker

Magical cheetahs leaping out of swirling golden portals may be a work of fiction, but Dr. Laurie Marker is a true wildlife hero.

Dr. Marker first traveled to Namibia, Africa in 1977. While she was there, she realized that there was a huge problem between the farmers and the cheetahs. Because the cheetahs were losing their habitat, they sometimes ate the farmer's livestock.

Dr. Marker tried to help the farmers understand how to live side by side with the cheetahs. It wasn't easy at first. Many people told her to go back home to America. But Dr. Marker believed that saving the cheetah was important. So important, that it became her life mission.

Dr. Marker moved to Namibia and in 1990 she founded the Cheetah Conservation Fund (CCF). Her center is responsible for research, education and finding ways to help farmers protect their animals with programs, such as her 'Livestock Guarding Dog Program'.

CCF also works with farmers who have cheetahs living on their land. Cheetahs are captured and many are released back into the wild.

However, CCF sometimes finds orphaned or injured cheetahs that can never go back to the wild because of their medical conditions. CCF provides a sanctuary, a safe home, with plenty of land for these cheetahs to live peacefully for the rest of their lives.

Dr. Marker and CCF do so many wonderful things to help save the cheetah from extinction, but they need help. They need our help.

Centers like CCF need donations to continue their research and create education programs. They need funds for equipment, medicine, and food for their orphaned and injured cheetahs.

You can make a difference. Visit the Cheetah Conservation Fund website at www.cheetah.org. Learn about CCF and see what kids are doing to help on their link 'You Can Help' – 'Kids for Cheetahs'.

The Wild Animals Kids Club series was written for kids just like you. Kids who love animals. Kids with the heart and courage to stand up for all of our endangered species.

Help CCF help Cheetahs with a donation and be sure to tell them that you're *A Wild Animal Kid!*

"I...am...Cheetah! The Gift" was inspired by my son's love for cheetahs and by wildlife heroes, like Dr. Laurie Marker.

A woman who dedicates her life to saving the cheetah.

A woman who continues to show the world that- *"Anything is possible...if you just believe!"*

~*About the Author*~

Stephanie J. Teer

Stephanie truly believes that a child's imagination is magical.

When her son, David, fell in love with wild animals, she began searching for fictional books that portrayed his favorite animal—The Cheetah!

After her search came up empty, she decided to write a book for her son...as a gift.

I...am...Cheetah! The Gift, is the first book in *The Wild Animal Kids Club* series. It's a series filled with humor, friendship, challenges, a bit of fantasy, and of course, the beauty of some of our planet's most endangered wild creatures.

What began as a gift for her son has now turned into a mission for Stephanie and her family. Each book in the series is dedicated to promoting real wildlife heroes that are making a difference for our endangered species.

Stephanie hopes that her books will encourage children to learn more about our planet's endangered animals. She also hopes that children will find creative ways to make a difference for the animals they love.

But mostly, she hopes that kids from around the world will continue

...to foster their imagination with creativity

...to believe that anything is possible

...and most importantly, to find the magic within themselves.

Learn more about Cheetahs!

Parents and teachers, visit the Cheetah Conservation Fund Center website at www.cheetah.org to help your children or students learn more about the cheetah.

Under the "About the Cheetah" link, click the "Educational Aides" and the "For Kids" tabs. There, you will find some wonderful educational resources for children of all ages.

Be sure to also take a look at Dr. Laurie Marker's beautifully illustrated book - *"A Future for Cheetahs"*.

From CCF Website:
Dr. Laurie Marker and noted wildlife photographer Suzi Eszterhas have teamed up to bring you the most intimate portrait yet of the world's fastest land animal, the cheetah in their upcoming book,
"A Future For Cheetahs"

For the first time, Dr. Marker shares the story of the cheetah's race against extinction, illustrated with some of the rarest and most beautiful images yet of the wild cheetah.

www.cheetah.org

*Connect with **WILD ANIMAL KIDS** on Facebook!*

A kid friendly site with wild animal news, coloring pages, events, and information on upcoming books in the Wild Animal Kids Club series.

https://www.facebook.com/WildAnimalKids

21688187R00098

Made in the USA
Middletown, DE
09 July 2015